MONSIGNOR WILLIAM BARRY MEMORIAL LIBRARY
BARRY UNIVERSITY
PS3559.R63 R37 1987
Irsfeld, John H., 1937-   010101 000
Rats alley / John H. Irsfeld.

0 2210 0111322 6

Y0-CJG-391

PS
3559   203887
.R63
R37
1987

Msgr. Wm. Barry Memorial Library
Barry University
Miami, FL 33161

IRSFELD

RATS ALLEY

Rats Alley

Other Books by John Irsfeld
Coming Through
Little Kingdoms

Rats Alley

· · · · · · · · · · · · · · · ·

John H. Irsfeld

University of Nevada Press

Reno & Las Vegas

Library of Congress Cataloging-in-Publication Data
Irsfeld, John H., 1937–
Rats alley.

I. Title.
PS3559.R63R37   1987   813'.54   86-14655
ISBN 0-87417-117-2 (alk. paper)

The paper used in this book meets the
requirements of American National Standard for
Information Sciences—Permanence of Paper
for Printed Library Materials,
ANSI Z39.48-1984.
Binding materials were chosen for strength and durability.
∞
University of Nevada Press, Reno, Nevada 89557 USA
Copyright © John H. Irsfeld 1987.
All rights reserved
Printed in the United States of America

This book is a fiction, "a making up of imaginary happenings," a transmogrification of the stuff of life into something that could have happened, or might have happened, in some cases into something that maybe even should have happened. The internal lives of the characters I have created and portrayed herein are creations of mine, not of nature. In short, I have not told what happened last summer but what happened next summer.

Dustjacket Illustration by Gary Freeman

> I think we are in rats' alley
> Where the dead men lost their bones.
>
> T. S. ELIOT
> *The Waste Land*

Joe Ben Strother

The van looked to me like it would go right through that big window in the front, but it wouldn't. It hit something more than just glass, I know that. Or I didn't have enough of a run at it, one. But I was scared to try it again, so I backed it around and hit on the side window, that moves, that they open to drive them in at.

It's not the one I would of bought from them, I know that much, but it wasn't that bad either. Only it's the only one I could get the keys from, to take it, after they'd all gone home. It did have a sunset painted on the side. Me and Steve was in there early in the afternoon, looking around as if we was going to buy it, or one of them other ones. Nobody really waited on us. They never do if you're a kid seventeen. They don't even like you to be in there. I told them my dad was outside with one of the salesmen, looking at a Diplomat. That settled them down some. I told them I was going into the marines on Monday and that as soon as I finished boot camp I was going to come back and get me one of them vans. They didn't believe that, which was closer to the truth than my daddy was outside fixing to buy him a Diplomat. He wouldn't drive nothing but a pickup truck, not even if you gave it to him. Maybe Mama's Oldsmobile, or a Cadillac.

So as soon as they realized we wasn't really going to buy nothing but that they probably ought not to kick us out because my daddy was outside, they pretty much left us alone. I climbed up in that van and sat behind the wheel like I was driving that thing. Then I got out and me and Steve went back into the waiting room, the service waiting room, and we got a drink of water and watched television a minute or two, golf I believe it was, and then we went back out and looked at one of the imports a little while. The second time up in it I realized the keys was still in the van. I mean, I think I knew it before, the first time, but I didn't realize what it meant. I hadn't thought of taking one off the showroom. I mean, the idea of going through the plate glass window, that big window, never occurred to me. Then I saw that everything on the lot had a lockbox on the window. *Everything* was locked up. The windows all rolled up tight. That's when I figured I'd go inside and see if there was any way I could get a lockbox key. But it was too busy; there was too much traffic in there, and I couldn't figure out where they kept those damn things. So I was sort of in limbo, you know. Sort of in a holding pattern, like they say, waiting for something. And the second time I was up in that van and I realized that the keys was there—right there in the ignition—then I knew exactly what I'd do.

I climbed down out of that thing and went to get Steve. He was back over at that little Jap car.

"Come on," I go. "Let's get out of this place."

"What?" he goes. "What happened? Somebody giving you some shit?"

"Naw," I go. "Just come on. Don't run. Just head for that door yonder." I pointed over at the side door and started toward it, slow and kind of bouncing, the way black dudes do. Steve was right with me when we went out the door. We was even bumping into each other getting out of there.

But we didn't run or cause any suspicion, because didn't anybody come after us hollering and yelling. We headed straight on out of the lot toward the street and then across to where Steve had parked his Camaro in the customers' parking lot.

"Take it easy going out," I said to him as we got to the car. I know Steve. He keeps that Chevy tuned like a son of a bitch and

I figured he'd want to gun the shit out of it when we left; lay a little rubber on them assholes, the way they treated us.

"What?" he said as he got in. "You sound just like my old man."

I could tell by the way he said it he was going to lay a strip all the way to the frontage road, so I ran around as fast as I could to the passenger's side to get in before he could get the son of a bitch started and in gear.

"You have been stuck in that one-horse town too long," he said. "And I don't think they take any pussies in the United States Marine Corps."

"Pussy?" I go, leaning across to him, over the console. "*Pussy?*" And I held my hand out so he could see. It took him a minute or two before it soaked in. He'd already cranked up the engine and had slipped the gear shift into low and was sounding his mufflers out.

You could see it all over his face when he finally got it. He started smiling, then he started grinning. Then he started laughing out loud.

"You son of a bitch!" he goes. "You son of a *bitch!*"

Steve Rainey

Joe Ben called me about eight-thirty, nine o'clock on Friday night. Lucky I was in. I ain't usually in on Friday night. He said him and another old boy was coming down to Houston from home. We all grew up together there. Joe Ben was two years behind me, but he was a good guy. We got along good. The other old boy was Wiley Brown. He was a senior, a year behind me.

Joe Ben had had a fight with Madeline, he said, a bad one. Joe Ben had kept telling her he was fixing to go into the marines on Monday and that she ought to, you know, let him do it. She kept saying that was about the dumbest thing she'd ever heard of, doing it with a guy that was taking off the next Monday and she might never see him again. He must really think she was dumb, or crazy. So he'd said fuck it, and had took her home and then gone and got Wiley out at the Dairy Queen. They had a couple of beers then, and went riding up the highway and back and then down and through the square, by the courthouse and the new jail there, that was built after the flood.

Then about eight-thirty or nine, somewhere in there, they'd decided they'd come down to see me. So they went to the phone in front of the U-Tote-M out on the highway and called. Like I say, it was lucky I was in, it being Friday night. Sometimes I don't stay and work on my car on Fridays. Sometimes I go out to Gilley's in Pasadena, or just ride up and down, drinking beer and listening to the radio, looking for stuff. But I was there at my place—my Aunt Bell's place, where I'm staying—working on my Camaro. Ever since I put that new carburetor on that thing I can't get it adjusted just right. It's always shutting down when I'm just starting across an intersection and I've got to get in a hurry or get "U.S. Post Office" or "Plymouth" or something like that bradded across my side door.

I was working in the garage, with that little electric heater on, because it was still getting cold in the evenings then. My aunt and her boyfriend had gone out, and I was home alone. The kids was sleeping over at some of their friends' house somewhere. I had the radio on, KIKK, loud country music, so it's lucky I even heard the phone. It started ringing during the hymn of the hour. I started not to answer it; I suredidn't think it would be for me. But it kept ringing so I finally did.

"Hello," I said.

"Steve?" said the voice at the other end.

"What?"

"Is this Steve Rainey?"

"Yes," I said. "Who wants to know?"

"This is Joe Ben," said the voice. At first I didn't know Joe Ben who, because I'd been down in Houston long enough, you know, since I graduated. Almost a year. So then he said, "Joe Ben Strother," and about the time he said that, I knew who it was.

Well, I was glad to hear from him. I'd been gone from home a long time, it seemed like, but not long enough that I'd made any friends, you know. I'd been working construction all day long and I'd come home, clean up, eat, watch TV, and then I'd go to bed. On Fridays I'd work on my car or go out to Gilley's. Saturdays I'd sleep late, watch the ballgame on TV, whatever it was. Maybe go to a movie. Or I'd baby-sit for my Aunt Bell so she and Buddy could go out somewhere. I don't know what I'd do on Sundays. Seems like it just went from Friday to Saturday to 7:00 A.M. Monday morning. I was making good money, though, I'll say that. But sometimes I missed home a lot, even my folks. So when Joe Ben called and said him and Wiley Brown was thinking about coming down to Houston, I said, "Sounds like a good idea to me."

And I asked him, "When?"

He said, "Right now."

I wasn't so sure about that at first, but then I thought, "Why not? I ain't going nowhere." So I said, "Well, come ahead on then."

"We'll see you in about four hours," he said.

"You walking?" I asked him.

"No. Same as walking. We taking Wiley's Chevrolet."

Then I could hear laughing and scuffling and cussing. Wiley don't like somebody to put his car down.

So I give Joe Ben my Aunt Bell's address and told him how to find the place and everything and then I hung up and went and got me a Budweiser and went back out to the garage to try to figure out how to adjust that goddamned butterfly valve on that goddamned carburetor.

I worked for a couple more hours and had me a few more beers. Then I went inside about eleven and took a shower and cleaned up again, from all the grease I got working on that damn Chevy. Then I got dressed and come out to the living room and watched TV a while.

I must of gone to sleep, though I didn't realize it, because I like to have broke my neck when my head popped back up straight all of a sudden because I heard someone at the door. At first I thought it was Joe Ben and Wiley but then I realized it wasn't when I heard the key in the lock. It was Aunt Bell and Buddy. I could see they was a little disappointed to see me sitting there on the sofa watching the TV. It was a good movie. John Wayne.

"I thought you might go out," said Aunt Bell.

I don't think I'm in her way. I mean, her and Buddy have been living together for a couple of years. It ain't that. I just think she worries about me, that I'd been there with her almost for a year and I didn't have a girl or no friends or nothing. I don't know what Buddy thought. Thinking ain't exactly a big point with Buddy.

"Joe Ben Strother called from home," I said. "Him and Wiley Brown is coming down tonight."

7

Aunt Bell sort of perked up at that. I think she missed home, too, sometimes.

"Reckon it'd be all right if they crashed here?" I asked. Buddy had already left the room. I could hear him from down the hall, taking a leak. He never shut the door. Or put the seat up, either, which was the one thing Aunt Bell purely hated.

"Sure," Aunt Bell said. "You know that. I'm glad to have them."

She put her purse over on the lamp table.

"Only don't you all be smoking any of that dope, you hear?"

"Yes, Aunt Bell," I said. I don't think she'd know it if we was. We'd just tell her we was smoking Mexican cigarettes. Might be, too.

She sat down with me and watched the end of the movie. I practically cried when John Wayne said he wouldn't give up all rights to his godson, little Robert William Pedro. Then the judge only put him in jail for a year. That was fair enough, considering he had sure enough robbed the bank there in Jerusalem. The best line was when Pedro had fell and broke his leg out in the Arizona desert. The other godfather, the kid, had already died. Pedro knew he was going to. He didn't have no water and his leg was broke. He asked John Wayne to leave his pistol with him. "On account of the coyotes," he said. "Yeah," John Wayne said, "on account of the coyotes," and then he started off with their godson heading back to the town of Jerusalem, just like in the Bible. Then, a few yards away, he stopped and said back to Pedro, "I'm sorry I called you a chili-dipping horse thief." And then he went on. A few hundred yards further away and then you could hear the gun go off, and you knew old Pedro hadn't shot any coyote; he'd shot himself.

Buddy never came back out. He disappeared into the bedroom.

After the movie was over, Aunt Bell said she'd be going to bed, too.

"Don't wait up too late for them," she said. "They might of stopped by the side of the road to get some sleep."

"That's right," I said. "I won't."

8

But it wasn't much longer after that they showed up. They was both about half-drunk, but so was I.

We went out and got something to eat and I remember how all wound up Joe Ben was about everything: Madeline and their fight they'd had, and his leaving school to go into the marines, his troubles with school and the law and his folks . . . just everything.

Then we went back to Aunt Bell's house and I made them pallets up on the floor because they said they'd rather sleep there than in the kids' beds.

"Ain't no telling what them kids might have," said Wiley.

"More than me," Joe Ben said, really sad, and I felt like I did when John Wayne fell down in the dust storm with that little baby in the movie and it looked like they was both going to die only he threw away the Bible and it turned to a page where he read it and it told him what to do.

Which I wish had happened to me and Joe Ben that night.

Madeline Higley

We did everything else together, Joe Ben and me, so I suppose it wouldn't have made any difference if we'd done that, too—gone ahead and done it. But somehow I just couldn't get over the idea that he was just using me. That he didn't really love me like he said he did. Not that I'm the one to be talking about that, I know. When I was fourteen I knew all about love, but at seventeen I'm not so sure. For one thing, I didn't always feel the same thing for Joe Ben. Sometimes I'd feel as if he was the most wonderful thing that ever happened to me. And Mama and Daddy both liked him, even though he'd had his troubles in school and with the police. My daddy used to say if he'd had a boy he wouldn't have minded a boy like Joe Ben. Parents are funny about that a lot of times, though. If a boy is polite, has good manners and is clean and everything, then they're likely to think he's a nice boy. Some of them are the very ones you take your life in your hands to go out with. Joe Ben wasn't, though. I'll say that for him. And I'm not just making that up now on account of what happened. Mama and Daddy liked him and he was a good boy. I could always control things with him. Until that last night, anyway. I guess I should have gone ahead. I might have, too, if he had waited until we had a chance to go out and park after the movie. I might have just gone ahead with the idea of seeing if I could keep him from going into the marines on Monday. But it was almost like he figured out the least likely way to get me to do it and then tried that way. Boys don't understand girls. If he'd just been tender and gentle and kind, and had touched me and kissed me the way he usually did, I might have done it. But the way he did it, the way he approached it, I didn't want to even kiss him or do it to him with my hand like we usually did. I just thought the whole idea of even being with him was repulsive.

"I think you are making a big mistake, Madeline," he said to me.

"And I think you're quite mistaken about me, too," I said.

We didn't talk for a while.

He lit a cigarette and looked out the car window. We were in his mother's Oldsmobile and he had the heater and the radio on so I said, "We'd better just go on to the show before you wear that battery down and your mama'll kill you."

"I'll tell you what let's do," he said real suddenly. "Let's just take you home where you'll be safe like little girls ought to be on Friday nights."

And he started the car up right away and backed around—we were out by the lake, just down from the new dam—and headed back into town.

I was so mad I could've spit. I didn't say a word. That's all I was to him, then, just somebody for sex. I swear boys think that's all girls are good for, doing something with their bodies to them, or having babies and going to the grocery store.

When he pulled up in front of our house he started to say something to me, I'm pretty sure. He turned off the engine and turned toward me real quick like he was getting ready to talk some more—make one last try, maybe, or maybe apologize. I don't think he was going to apologize. I certainly can't think he was going to apologize. For if that's what he was going to do, or if I'd gone ahead and done it with him, then things might have been different. But I can't think that way. And there's no one I can even tell what we really quarreled about. And everyone's saying what a good, fine young man he was. He was.

But I never gave him a chance to say a word. I opened the door as fast as I could and got out and slammed it right in his face and I never said a thing myself. I guess I felt pretty good about that at the time, but I don't now.

I just wish I'd gone ahead and done it with him and then maybe the worst thing that would of happened was he would of gone off into the marines and I would of got pregnant and had a baby. Because at least then I would of had something good out of all of it.

He peeled rubber going away from my house, and the sound of it startled me because the night was so quiet and it made the little hairs on the back of my neck stand up. They are standing up right now as I remember that night and everything else.

And nobody told me anything until Tuesday of the next week.

Eldon "Chow-Chow" Kaprow

. . . .

    Friday night and she has to go to her mother's to be with all of them and she knows I don't go out on Friday nights when I have the Saturday night shift. I don't know what's wrong with that son of a bitch anymore. At least she still cleans up the house and cooks the meals. But I swear to God she's been watching Jane Fonda or somebody on that fucking TV set. Something's put a burr under her saddle, that's for sure. She don't like me touching her anymore. I know that. I know she don't know I know that, too. She don't think I know much at all. Just a dumb cop, is what she thinks. Maybe so. Maybe that *is* all I am. But I know something else, too: she's not the only one that thinks there might be something wrong with this marriage. It ain't all that hot to fuck somebody you know don't want to fuck you. Even if she does cook all the meals and do the laundry, like she's supposed to. She never looked at it from my side. I'm not that excited about suiting up everyday and going out there to be fucked with by everybody as if I was part of an occupying army and not on their side, protecting their asses. Cops got feelings, too. And we ain't all as dumb and insensitive as they think we are; even her, Linda.

    It was great when we first met, I'll never forget that. When I was just out of the Corps and she and those other girls came into the Smokehouse that night and me and Jimmy were there eating supper and drinking Shiner beer. I hadn't been out more than a week, I remember that. And Jimmy knew Linda and those other girls, I can't call their names after so many years, and he invited them over to sit with us. We pulled another table next to ours and got them chairs and sat there while they ate and we all drank a lot more beer and then I remember we went out to Lukash's dance hall and danced and drank beer until they closed.

I liked Linda from the first. We were in the back seat of Jimmy's car. He was driving and the other two girls were in the front seat with him. It was October, but it wasn't cold yet. Jimmy was driving a Ford then, and there was more room in the front seat of that thing than there was in the back. Not that Linda and I minded, though; we didn't. We had to sit kind of sideways because my legs are so long. Linda sort of curled up beside me on the seat. I don't know. We necked a lot that night, and I really tried to get her to do it, but she held out against me. I'm glad now she did. I wouldn't have respected her if she hadn't. She didn't hold out too long, though, and that was good, too. Because if she had, I would of just quit calling her. She let me touch her boobs that night, but wouldn't let me put my hand on her pussy. She was horny, too, I remember that.

"You want to," I said to her.

"Yes," she said, "I do. But I'm not going to."

"But why not?" I said. "What could it hurt?"

"I don't know," she said. "We'll have to wait and see."

So Jimmy and me took them all to Linda's house where they were staying. They were all in school then at Sam Houston and the two girls had worked there in town during the summer with Linda. So she'd brought them back home for the weekend.

I talked to her before she left to go back to school, but only on the phone. I didn't see her again that weekend. So then, about Tuesday, I got so I knew I had to see her again, I had to keep after her until I got her into the sack. I just couldn't get her out of my mind. What they call love, I guess. I call it just being horny. But God! Where it can get you. Of course, then I called it love, too, or something like it. Whatever it was, I called Jimmy Tuesday night and asked him where she lived over at Huntsville and he told me he didn't know but he'd find out. He called me back about thirty minutes later and gave me her address and phone number. I stewed around for a long time trying to make up my mind whether to call her and tell her I was coming up, or ask her if it was all right. But in the end I didn't call. I was afraid to. Subject feared rejection. You can't tell. She grew up right there in Schulenburg, so she'd been around Czechs all her life. I don't know how I missed knowing her; I guess I was just too old. She must of been a little girl when I went away. I worked a couple of years here in Houston and then I joined the Corps. I was gone away more than six years. In the meantime Linda got grown up. Went through high school and was gone off to college by the time I met her. She was a sophomore up there at Huntsville, majoring in English.

Looking back now after all this time I guess it would of been better if I hadn't gone up, but I did. I borrowed Daddy's car for I didn't have one yet and I drove up on Wednesday. I didn't have the nerve to call her that first day, but I talked myself into it on Thursday. I knew if I was going to get a date with her that weekend, then Thursday was the absolute last day I could call. Subject was also afraid she wouldn't remember him.

She did though.

"Oh," she said. "I thought I might be hearing from you."

I thought that was a little forward; I was used to being around girls who would have said, "Why, what a surprise." Except for whores, of course, either over at the Chicken Ranch in La Grange, or down on the border, or out in Okinawa where I pulled all my time. The Corps wasn't so bad. Only that's where I got it in my mind I was going to be a cop. Somebody should of stopped me right away, I can see that now. I think that's mostly what Linda hates. She is too sensitive for this kind of life. We're shit on like we were slaves or niggers and then they don't pay us shit for doing it, either. Letting them.

I know one thing: you couldn't get any of them cocksuckers who bad-mouth us so much to strap on a weapon every day and go out there and lay their goddamned life on the line for the piss-ant wage they pay us to do it. Only I ain't complaining. Some, I guess.

So I asked her for a date.

"Sure," she said. "I'd love to go out."

I see now, looking back, what made her interested in me. I was twenty-five, world-experienced at least upside those kids she was in college with. I wasn't that bad-looking. Most of all, though, I had got to reading novels when I was in the Corps. A guy I was stationed with who was my roommate for two years, a sandy-headed guy from El Paso, he read all the fucking time. I think that's *all* he did, besides pull his duty, because he never said shit and he never ate chow. Never slept much, either, now that I think of it. That's all the son of a bitch did, was read. He read all kinds of shit, too: novels, science books, newspapers, anything. It was like he was addicted to it the way a drug addict gets addicted to his drug. And he read all kinds of novels, too, good ones and bad ones both, though I didn't know there was a difference until I started going with Linda and she told me what was what. I can understand that, I guess, but I don't understand the standards in deciding. I can see how a Smith and Wesson is a superior handgun to an old Ivers and Johnson. It don't take much sense to figure that out. But I can't see that about a novel. The best I can tell is do I like it or don't I like it. That's it, except the ones Linda told me about.

We went out Friday night, Saturday night, and Sunday night. Saturday night we screwed for the first time. I say *fucked*. She says *made love*. Our compromise—*my* compromise, because she won't make one at all—is *screwed*.

I took Daddy's car home Sunday night. On Monday I packed what little shit I owned and moved over to Huntsville. I got a job as a security guard on a construction site first, because I had my own gun and leather. I started college that spring on the GI Bill, majoring in criminal justice. Linda got pregnant that spring, too, and so in June she and I got married in Schulenburg. We got married in a Catholic church, even though neither one of us was a very good Catholic. We've raised the kids that way, too, in the Church but just barely.

Pretty soon she got pregnant again, and after two years I had to drop out of school. I'd taken the tests to get on the force in Huntsville, but they had a waiting list as long as I am and nothing happened. I was working as a security guard again then and driving a taxi during the day, which isn't exactly how you make a killing in Huntsville. But it was more than the GI Bill and Linda couldn't work because of the children and I didn't want her to anyway. I figured that was my obligation the same as I do now.

In the summer of the third year we'd been married I took the tests for patrolman on the Houston Police Force, which I knew at the time it was the craziest thing I'd ever done with my life, including the Corps. Everybody knows about Houston. You can get murdered quicker here than anywhere in the United States, I believe, except maybe for Detroit or Las Vegas. For some reason, I don't know what it is, people here kill other people for the same things they just give each other the finger for in other places. I mean it. Al says it's the melting pot. He says there are so many different breeds of people here, blacks, chicanos, yankees, cajuns, you name it, that the only way you can melt them all down into one is to kill off everybody who resists melting. I don't go along with all of that. That's just some more of that college shit he throws around, I believe. I think sending a Mexican to college like Ruiz is just about as dangerous as sending a Czech like me. We're not ready for it, yet. It just makes us dissatisfied.

Only I wasn't dissatisfied at all until I figured out how dissatisfied she was. It's funny how that works. Like you don't mind dealing with a prosecutor or his witnesses or the grand jury or anything, because you know you and them have got the same goals and everything. But you do mind—excuse me, *Whereas* you do mind screwing with the defense attorney, all the bullshit they come up with. I mean, we wouldn't arrest the motherfuckers if we didn't think they was guilty. What do they think, we've just got quotas? They do, I know it.

We just want justice. That's it, though; nobody else wants it but just us. Ruiz says I'm full of shit about that. Strunk says I'm just a typical honky. Not only that, he says I stole that line from some nigger comedian, I don't know who. I've never stolen nothing. I've never crossed the law, ever. I've been a good citizen all my life. I never even goofed-off, hid out and slept in the laundry room or anything, when I was in the Corps. I never even laughed when they made jokes about it, like the Crow, the

Ball, and the Mudhook, or whatever it was. I've done everything I was ever supposed to do. And look where it's got me.

Where it's got me is home alone on Friday night, fixing up my uniform for tomorrow. I've clipped all the loose strings, run Magic Marker around my stripe edges, aligned my nameplate, polished my footgear. Everything. I am outstanding.

Except I called Linda's folks' house a while ago and talked to her mother and the kids. Linda's not there. She went out for a while. I know you can't get into too much trouble in Schulenburg on a Friday night. That's not the point. The point is I know something's eating on her. The point is I know she wishes she had stayed in school and gotten her degree, hadn't had four kids, wasn't married. None of it. The point is, *I* met her in Schulenburg on a Friday night, at the Smokehouse, and she could just as easily be meeting someone else there right now, some young hard-dicked twenty-five-year-old son of a bitch just out of the Corps horny as hell and looking for someone to fuck. And who knows, maybe she is looking, too. She's bound to be horny her ownself for all the fucking she hasn't been doing with me.

So, what the hell. It's Friday night and my gear's ready. I can't stay up too late or I'll sleep too late in the morning and then I won't be able to take a nap early tomorrow evening before I go on duty. So I guess I'll just sit here and have a few beers and watch the TV a while. There's a good movie on tonight called *The Three Godfathers* starring John Wayne. It's a western, I think. Old. I don't know, but I'll bet it doesn't glorify crime and the mob the way that Marlon Brando movie did, that other Godfather movie.

So I think I'll stay up and watch it and see if maybe I can't learn something that will make it easier for me in this life. Maybe John Wayne will show me which way do I go.

Alonzo Ruiz

It was bad enough in Weslaco.
Here it is pure natural hell, as Strunk would say.
At least in the Valley there are chicanos all over the place. You don't feel quite so alone. Like Strunk says, being stuck in River Oaks after dark make you feel like a fool. Dangerous, too. They'd shoot your ass in a minute down there. I'd rather be in Fifth Ward even if I'm not black like Strunk.

I went to school as usual last night. I may be a hundred years old before I get that degree, but I am going to get it. Then I can get out of this uniform and be a class lawyer and call myself *licenciado* in the Yellow Pages in the phone book.

Not that that's going to make that much difference in my life, though, I know that. There are still always going to be *pinche bofón* son of a bitches like that *puta rubia* in class.

She don't even know I heard her.

"All Mexicans want to do is rape white women." Who does that *fea canija* think she is? I wouldn't shit on a white woman. I told Strunk that. "That's not true, strictly speaking," he said. "You've shit on a lot of white women."

That's true, too. I do have a thing for them. Their little *panochas* with the blond hairs and the lips all so pinkish brown. Not better than a black *panocha*, a *latina*; just different.

I swear I can't get enough of that stuff. But last night I sure tried; and I'm going to try some more this morning, and that's the by-God truth. She was late last night. She didn't call or anything.

So after that fucking English composition class last night, I couldn't get away fast enough. I swear the University of Houston is going to be the death of me. I should of been born rich; then I could go to night school at Rice, ha ha. I don't know. We see as many of those kids screwing up as we do kids from Cougar High. Only we don't see as many of them going to jail. They ain't stupid; they wasn't born poor like some of us.

Poor isn't that bad, though. Dad worked his butt off as a plumber in Weslaco, but it was good honest work. I didn't know we was poor until I grew up and left home and joined the army. Nobody ever tells me anything. I remember the time I was helping Dad in the summer during school vacation. He got a call from this rich family of chicanos. I don't know where they made their money, doing what. They thought they were hot shit, though, I knew that. I'd heard about them even before we showed up there that day. The Rodriguez family, for Christ's sake. They lived in an anglo neighborhood, the whole nine yards. A little girl answered the door; she wasn't much younger than I was at the time, I remember that. I was about sixth or seventh grade.

"We're here to fix the sink," my Dad said, good old Señor Ruiz, father of the future *licenciado,* destined to become even worse than that little girl's family.

"Mama!" she yelled, that little black-eyed girl. "Some Mexicans are here to fix the sink."

I wanted to kill her. Just grab her and strangle her. I looked at my father to see how upset he was. He wasn't angry at all. His eyes were just sad and old. I was humiliated, for him and for myself. I remember I just turned around and went back to the truck and waited for him there. I wouldn't have gone in that house for a million dollars. He never said a word when he came out. We drove home in silence. But that night I heard him and Mama whispering to each other in their bedroom, separated from ours by only a hanging drape. And it wasn't little *palabras de amor* they were whispering either. I could tell the difference by then. It was about what happened that day and how my dad was worried that I wasn't waking up to the real world very fast. It must be a bitch to have to watch tiny children that you love, your own flesh and blood, waking up to the realization that there are people out there who will hate you desperately for no greater reason than that your skin is a different color than theirs is. Of course, it cuts both ways. I know brown brothers who hate black brothers, and I know brown and black who hate white. And then, of course, there's Kaprow, who hates everybody. He's not superficial about his hate, though. He doesn't hate because of skin color. He hates because of skin contents. It's the fact that there's a human being inside every one of those skins that upsets Chow-Chow so much. He said he got that nickname from that hot Bohemian relish, chow-chow. Strunk says he got it from being twice as mean as any single Chow dog around. I don't even think he knows he's as mean as he is. I remember that time we busted that one dude—white, too—who started giving Kaprow some lip about something and so Kaprow never said a word to him—no warning, no rights, nothing—but just reached up with that service revolver and hit him right on the lips with the bottom of the barrel. It looked like the barrel was a finger placed to his lips to say "sshhhh." I remember being terrified; the gun could have gone off and run a bullet right up that kid's nose and out the top of his head, taking his brains right with it, of course. Of course, too, if he'd had any brains he could have seen by looking at Kaprow to keep his mouth shut. We was all in on that one, together where our zones meet.

That scared me. I told Strunk and he said he used to ride with Kaprow and that's one reason he asked to be changed. He said Kaprow had stories circulating about him in Fifth Ward. "I be killing my own damn self, if I stay riding with that sucker," Strunk said.

So Strunk got his black ass transferred and then I ended up riding with him. Kaprow wasn't pissed off at him, I'll give him that. He never acted any different toward Strunk or me either one afterwards. He was still shitty to us. "He's an even-tempered sucker," says Strunk. "He's always mad. For a while there it looked like maybe he was going to be riding by himself, but then they scrounged up that no-account son of a bitch Jerry Winkleman. Though I'd like to know what rock they got him out from under. Kaprow is mean-tempered and he don't like people very much, but at least he's pretty smart. You figure if you're working for him you won't get your ass killed through terminal stupid combined with rednecked mean. That's Winkleman. It's hard to say the difference about their meanness. It's easy about their brains. I heard Kaprow's Marine Corps GT was 121. I believe it. I never heard nothing about Winkleman's. But I'd guess him at about 70. I'm not a snob about that. I know those things are written by Native White Protestants for Native White Protestants. Because I *know* mine's higher than 118, no matter what those *gringo cabrones* say. Anyway, Kaprow is twice as smart as Winkleman.

It's his meanness I can't say the difference about. Kaprow just don't like nobody, or at least that's how he acts. It's almost as if he was preoccupied with something on his mind all the time and every time he has to have something to do with another human being, like talk to him, or even see him, as far as that goes, he gets all irritated and pissed off. He looks more like a redneck than Winkleman does: that big bull-neck, his silly-ass flattop haircut. Strunk and me really pissed him off that day when we told him even George Jones had let his hair grow out. Blond-headed, too. Eyebrows look like caterpillars getting ready to crawl over to that big broken nose and head south. Winkleman looks like a rat to me. I suppose he looks like a redneck, too, but he looks more like a plain old rat to me. Strunk says he looks like a rat that smells something bad.

Me and Strunk have been together a long time, now, almost a year. So Winkleman and Kaprow will be a year come hot weather, just about. Anyway, we've driven that area, all of us, for many months now. It ain't been beer and skittles, but I think it will make me a better *licenciado*. I had always thought I'd do criminal defense, but after all these years as a cop, I don't know. Most of the guys feel like I do: they are fucking up or we wouldn't be bringing their asses in. Strunk and I both get more shit from our people than Kaprow or Winkleman do from theirs. Ours haven't figured it out yet: it's better to be inside the tent pissing out, than to be outside the tent pissing in.

Maria moves beside me now.

She likes that I call her Maria, *gringa* that she is. She was late coming over last night. I know she gets off at midnight. But I watched all of that goddamn John Wayne movie and then screwed around squaring away the kitchen before I went to bed. "Don't be talking Mexican in front of the kid!" he yelled at Pedro. It's hard to understand. He loved Mexico. One or two of his wives were Mexicans, for God's sake. Well, there's no accounting. I read he had put on his tombstone: *Feo, Fuerte, y Formál*. Don't be writing Mexican on the front of your tombstone! Well, I don't give a fuck. They can all go to hell.

She tried to slip into bed without waking me up, once she decided I was asleep, but I woke up the minute I heard the key in the lock. Maybe if she was here every night, lived here, I'd get used to it. But just the weekends ain't enough to make it a habit. So I didn't move or anything. Just lay quiet and kept breathing slow. Good stakeout practice. She undressed so quietly, all I could hear was the whisper of cloth and the purr of zippers. Then she slipped into bed so gently I never even felt a ripple in the waterbed over on my side.

After a few minutes she slid over toward me and bellied up against my back and I very gently reached up and just kept her hand moving over my side and down, closing her fingers around my hard cock. Because just hearing that son of a bitch undress in the dark turned me on so I could hardly stand it. I don't know how long it will be before that stops. What they called in that zoology class I had to take for a science requirement "pair bonding." All animals do it, I guess. I can't remember a year ago that good. You get your pair bonded by fucking your ass off. Then you indulge in what that professor called pair maintenance. Just keeping it from falling apart before your eyes, I guess. We pair bonded like mad fiends last night. Although I'm not sure still why she was in so late. I never said anything about it. In fact, I never said anything to her at all.

That's not why she's here. In fact, I don't even care where she was. I won't care, anyway.

She's moving again, waking up. And I am fixing—as Strunk would say—I am fixing to do me some pair bonding with one blonde-headed *gringa* son of a bitch, right on top of all that pair bonding from last night.

"*Oye, Maria,*" I say softly, lips against her ear, the wisps of blonde hair between us rougher than her skin, "*Maria, se acabó la noche. Es el tiempo ahora a mamar mi verga.*" She loves my sweet nothings even though she understands them no better than anything else in life except hustling cocktails and pair bonding.

"Hmmm," she says and Saturday morning begins.

Joe Ben Strother

. . . .

After I'd got the keys out of that van I still wasn't a hundred percent sure what I wanted to do, go back and take it or not. That morning when we woke up—it was about ten o'clock or so, around in there—Wiley claimed he had a hangover, though I don't know what from. Like, we never drank that much beer Friday night. And he goes, "I'm supposed to be at work at three," and I go, "Call in sick," and he goes, "Naw, I don't think so." And in thirty minutes he's in that damn Chevrolet of his and gone. I think he was just scared of being gone from home. I think he must have felt as if he didn't get back in the pen right away something terrible might happen to him. So he left and then Steve and I went out to get some breakfast and then we went riding around in Houston, just looking at things. Houston is big. You can ride around for hours and be right in the middle of town and never see the same place twice except the big buildings.

We were at a stoplight on Kirby somewhere—I couldn't have found my way to the ship channel at that point—and this van pulls up beside us.

"I'd like one of them things," I said to Steve.

"They get lousy mileage," he said.

"I know," I said. "But they're great for partying."

That didn't do me any good to think of that, though. I just commenced thinking of Madeline and how little I must mean to her that she'd let me go off to the marines on Monday without nothing to remember her by. No seal on our love.

Not that I really wanted to go into the marines, anyway. After I'd talked Mama and Daddy into signing for me, I came to the conclusion that I didn't really want to go into the service as bad as I just wanted to get my way with them—again. I can't say I'd gotten into all that trouble I had because of that—them spoiling me—but I can't see how it helped much, either. The trouble with that is when I wanted something I never thought about whether it was spoiling me or not spoiling me or whether it was good for me or not. I just wanted whatever it was I wanted, that's all. And they usually gave in to me. I guess it's because they're older and I'm the only one they've got. It can't be so I'll love them. They know I love them, no matter what they do.

A little while later, then, Steve and me went to the Dodge place and walked around out in the lot for a while. That's when I really started getting the idea. I mean I had this picture of me driving back home in a van—I got that when we seen the van at the stoplight. But about the time we got out on that lot I had gone from wishing I could buy one to knowing I couldn't and being pissed off about it, to thinking, "Well, fuck them. I'll just take one of the son of a bitches any damn way. Drive it home and then wipe off all my prints and leave it there." But all the cars—vans and everything—were locked up on the lot. So me and Steve went inside. And that's when I seen them keys and got the idea about just taking that one off the show-window floor.

After we left the place and I had the keys Steve quieted down a lot. At first he laughed his ass off. Then he got real quiet and I could tell he was worried about what I'd done, what I was fixing to do.

"Look," I go. "Your name won't even come into it, even if they do catch me, which they won't."

"Don't be too sure," he goes. "These Houston cops are something else. You ain't fucking around with Sheriff Wilson here. These guys will beat the shit out of you. You know what they done to a Mexican here just a while back? They beat the shit out of that son of a bitch and threw his ass into Buffalo Bayou."

I go, "So?"

"So, he died, that's *so*."

I shrugged my shoulders. I ain't no Mexican. They wouldn't pull no shit like that on a white dude.

"And two of the cops who done it was Mexicans their own-selves."

I shrugged my shoulders again, but I didn't feel quite so cocky about it that time. That did mean something. If a Mexican cop would do that to another Mexican . . . well, it just didn't seem right.

We decided we'd go to a dirty movie then. We had to kill some time before it got late enough to go back and break in that place and get the van and drive it out of there. We never would, I knew. There would be alarms all over that damn place. So we went back toward town.

"There's one of these places out near Post Oak," Steve goes. "But I like the ones downtown better. They're raunchier, plus sometimes there will be a whore in there, and you can get a blow-job or a hand-job."

That would show Madeline, I thought. If I could get me a blow-job in the dirty movie in Houston. Then maybe she wouldn't be so quick to say no every time I asked her to let me do it. Not that I'd have any more chances to ask her that, at least for a while, considering the fact that I was leaving town on Monday to join the marines. I'd already got the papers signed for being underage. They were at home, so I had to go back and get them anyway. My old man was going to be really pissed off at me for not coming home last night or tonight either, but he wouldn't give me too much shit, I figured, considering I was leaving on Monday.

I felt the keys to that van. They were in my pocket and they felt like they weighed about ten pounds. It made my stomach quiver and the bottoms of my feet tingle to think about what I intended to do after a while. It made me feel the same way to think about going into the marines on Monday. I didn't really want to take that van, but I couldn't see how I could get out of it now.

We parked the Camaro near the dirty movie theater on Main and paid our money and went inside. It smelled like a mixture of come and Lysol in there. There was an orgy on the movie screen when we went in, eight or nine men and women hooked up with each other all kinds of different ways.

I didn't really want to go into the marines on Monday, either, but I didn't see how I could get out of that without sure enough being a chicken. Of course, it wasn't Monday morning yet, and things have a way of happening sometimes to save you from shit you don't want to do.

Ben Strother

. . . .

I worked late yesterday evening trying to get the stock straightened out some. The way people come in and move things around from one place to another you would think they do it on purpose. Part of it is being in that shopping center, I know, on the edge of town, like in a big city. A lot of folks come over from Fort Hood now, I believe, since we've got that big Buddy's Supermarket in. They think they're going to save some money. I understand a lot of things are just as cheap or cheaper than they are in the commissary there on the post. But still, after you add the expense of driving over, I don't see how they can save much. On the other hand, maybe it's just for something to do.

I wondered where that boy was, but I decided against calling the Higleys and asking them if Madeline was missing, too. Or late. I guess if she was they would of been calling me, since it was Joe Ben she was out with. Doreen was never even upset about it all last evening. He'd stayed out that late before. Something was different, though. I don't believe in psychic experiences or any of that stuff, but I did just have a feeling that something wasn't right. I did wonder where he was, and I usually don't do that at all. Usually I push it out of my mind; I just don't want to know what he's up to.

Doreen had waited supper for me. The boy had already gone out on his date with Madeline. Nice girl. Doreen hardly eats anything anymore anyway. She had a good supper. There were pork chops cooked in mushroom gravy, which I really like, and pinto beans with onions and fat meat, and greens. She always has been a good cook. She learned from her grandmother in Corsicana who raised her. The inside of Doreen's refrigerator right now looks like it belongs to someone of two generations ago. She cans, jars, everything. She cooks everything from scratch. That yankee pharmacist at the drugstore out at the shopping center, the soldier's wife. She never says *cooks*, she always says *makes*. "I've got to make supper when I get home." "I made roast beef last Sunday." I never say nothing to her. It's not my place. It's just funny to me how people from different places say different things like that. The same with food. Yankees look down on black-eyed peas, for example. They call them cow peas in some places, I've heard, and they feed them to the cattle. I call that wasteful. There's no accounting. But I guess that's what makes America the wonderful country it is. Or at least used to be. Nowadays, who can be sure? We seem like we want to just give everything away as fast as we can: all our money, all our wheat, all our power. And I don't know about all this energy business, either. All this oil. When I was a boy coming up we paid thirteen, fourteen cents a gallon for gasoline. Now it's more than a dollar. Nobody can tell me there isn't something wrong with that, for it just to come all of a sudden like that in one short period of time.

We ate supper. I was already thinking about the boy. Somehow—like I say, I don't believe in any of that psychic stuff—but somehow I had already started worrying about him. That isn't right; it wasn't worry yet. But he was surely on my mind, and I was thinking about him. Partly, of course, it was because Doreen and I had signed that consent agreement form for him to go into the service even though he wasn't eighteen yet. I guess even now I feel like maybe as soon as I signed that I sort of turned him loose for the world to get hold of. I know that's crazy, too. The world already had gotten several cracks at him.

"Are those pork chops all right?" Doreen asked. She had that kind of sad look in her eyes she'd been getting lately, ever since the boy had taken those hubcaps that time and had got caught. I guess if it hadn't of been for Sheriff Wilson being the kind of man he is, the boy would have gone to jail then. Maybe he should have. No. That's not right; it wouldn't have done any good to do that.

"Yes," I said. "They're just fine, Doreen. So are the greens and the pinto beans," I added, for I knew she would ask me about each thing if I didn't say something first.

The trouble is, he's just like all the kids are nowadays. At least most of them. I can't even see where the student body presidents are any different than the usual kids nowadays. Maybe it's the television. Or something we done wrong, as their parents. Though I don't know how else to do than what we done. We punished him for bad grades and for getting in trouble at school. When I bought him that car last year and he wrecked it, then I never bought him a new one. I told him if his grades come up we'd talk about it. But they never come up. And he's not a dumb boy, either, I told him. That counselor at school, I can't remember his name, he told me the boy had a good IQ; over average. He was no genius, he said, but he was above average.

Of course, maybe that was the problem. I met a lot of guys like him when I was in the service. Old boys who had just enough intelligence to be over average, just enough to always be getting into trouble. It was like people like that are just smart enough to be dissatisfied, but not smart enough to do anything about it. They spend too much time thinking about themselves, I think.

"There's more of everything," Doreen said. But I'd had enough. I'm at that age where I have to watch everything I eat; it all turns straight to fat on me. I don't want to die of a heart attack like my daddy.

So Doreen cleaned up the kitchen then and I sat there at the table and smoked a cigarette and talked to her about my day.

It was late when she was through and there wasn't much on television we wanted to watch, so we turned on the radio instead and got one of them big powerful stations in Fort Worth–Dallas and listened to it for a while. I read the paper and Doreen worked on her needlepoint, which I swear to God is going to make that woman blind. We went to bed around ten-thirty or eleven, which is right late for us. I dozed off right away, but then I woke up within the hour. Doreen seemed to me like she was sound asleep.

I knew it was too early for the boy, but I was wondering where he was, what he was doing; why me and Doreen had signed that paper. The house seemed awfully empty all of a sudden, with him out of it and the idea that after Monday he'd be out of it more or less forever. Because after a boy's gone off to service, he comes back grown up and then things are different. Or he doesn't come back.

I was tossing and turning by then and I was worried I was going to wake Doreen up so I got out of bed and put on my bathrobe and went out to the living room. It was pretty chilly in the house, so I turned the thermostat up again and then I fixed myself some ice cream with chocolate that I found in the refrigerator. I tried to read for a while but I couldn't get interested in anything, so I started looking around for something to do.

I never went through the boy's stuff; and I didn't that night. But I did go into his room and turn on the light and look around. I saw all those pictures of him when he was younger. There used to be baby pictures in there but he made his mother take them down. They embarrassed him when his friends came over, he said. I can see that, though his mother couldn't. His room was neat, though I know he never left it that way. His mother came in after he left on his date and cleaned it up for him. His bed was made and the covers turned down for him. She always did that for that boy. I always thought that expressed her love for him as much or more than anything else she done for him. And she done everything.

I saw on the corner of his desk the jigsaw puzzle he'd gotten along with a hundred other things for Christmas. For some reason, I don't know why really, I went over and picked it up. It was a peculiar puzzle. It wasn't a picture of a scene, you know, a boat at rest in a harbor, or a mountain, or a European villa, nothing like that. It was just yellow pencils, yellow wooden pencils like you see all the time. They were all generally pointing down toward the bottom of the picture with their erasers at the top, but they were crossed over each other, too, some of them, at slight angles. I never work those damn things. I don't even like them. But I couldn't sleep, and I didn't feel like reading, and before I'd even really thought about it, I had opened up that puzzle and dumped it out on the boy's desk and had started sorting the edge pieces out.

The next time I looked at my watch it was three-thirty in the morning. I had gotten all the edge pieces out and done most of the border. It took me a few minutes to realize what was bothering me about everything and then I got it. There I was in the boy's room, and he wasn't in it and it was three-thirty in the morning.

"Well," I told myself. "He's been out this late before." And, "After all, he's going away on Monday and this is his last big weekend with his girlfriend."

I knew I should be going to bed. Still, I thought I'd work on that pencil puzzle a little more. My body was tired, but my mind wasn't. It was going like crazy. I was thinking a lot of things I hadn't thought of in years. It had been years, too, since I had stayed up like that.

Because I was worried about the boy. I was worried he wasn't in and I was worried about him going into the marines. I just didn't think he was strong enough for that.

And so I worked on the puzzle until I could see it start breaking light outside, through the boy's bedroom window. And then I knew if I was going to get even a couple of hours, I'd better go back to bed and do it.

I turned out the light in the boy's bedroom. It was light enough outside by then that I could make out the enlargement of his junior class picture that his mother had made and then framed and hung on the bedroom wall. He was right thin then; he'd gained a little weight since the early fall when it was taken. His blond hair was too long for my tastes even though it was still too short for his. I'd loved to see him that next Monday or whenever it was when that Marine Corps barber got through with him.

I loved that boy. I don't guess I turned out to be the greatest father in the world, judging how he turned out. But I'm still convinced everything would have been all right if . . .

Well, there's no point in dwelling on it. It didn't. And I knew from the start something was wrong that night.

Doreen was still breathing like she was asleep and I felt very protective of her. For some reason I felt sorry for her, too, and kind of superior. As if I was in on some great terrible secret that she didn't know about and so I had to save up my strength in order to protect and care for her when she found out. And I was right.

Doreen Strother

I heard Ben come to bed.

I don't think he slept at all. I didn't sleep as good as I usually do because I was worried about Joe Ben. But I knew I'd better sleep because I might need it.

As soon as I knew Ben was asleep I went ahead and got up. It was Saturday morning but I knew the church would be open anyway. Reverend White has been keeping it open all day every day since he got the call here.

I dressed quietly so I wouldn't wake Ben up and then I went over to the church. Joe Ben had my car and so I walked. I don't like to drive Daddy's pickup truck. I never even went down the hall to see if Joe Ben was in because I knew he wasn't. I wasn't surprised that my car wasn't there, either. Anyway, it's only four blocks over to the church. No one was there but me. I sat about in the middle and I prayed for the longest time. I would have felt better praying on my knees but we don't do that. It's funny about that; Catholics do and I think Episcopalians do. So I guess that's the reason us Baptists don't. I would have felt more like I was praying. I started out good, but then I kept drifting off the subject and thinking about Joe Ben, what a wonderful baby he was and how thankful I was to the Lord for blessing me at my age. Ben and I had wanted children and we had tried for years. I used to get furious with those women on television who were lobbying for abortions when I couldn't even get pregnant. I wanted to go to the doctor to see what was wrong, but Ben wouldn't hear of it. I knew it was my fault, not his, but I think maybe he was afraid it was his. Then finally I did get pregnant and Joe Ben was born and there were no complications or anything. I was so proud it was a boy, too, for I was sure that's what Ben wanted even though he said as long as I was all right he didn't care what it was.

He loved that baby from the start. He was a good daddy, too, although I blame both of us for spoiling that boy. That's how Ben talked me into signing that consent paper with him, even though only one of us really needed to, I think. Because, he said, maybe the service could make up for where we went wrong, were too easy on the boy. I never thought we were that much too easy. When he wrecked that car Daddy bought him he wouldn't get him another one. I thought that was fairly hard on him.

When he was just a baby I could hold him next to my heart and I could feel his little heart beating and he would lie there and smile up at me so sweetly; then he started walking and talking and after that everything just got out of my control. But I don't see how we had time to do wrong by him. Seventeen years isn't anything. Seventeen years is just a baby.

I didn't want to pray for anything, but I couldn't help that either. I mainly just wanted to praise the Lord that maybe in His bounty He would see fit to bless us and let my little boy come home all right. But I couldn't even do that right, either. I kept asking Him to let Joe Ben be all right and to let him come home and then thanking Him, too, for his Grace, in between times.

Take me, I said, in his place, if you want to. After a while I got so hungry and my stomach was growling so loud that I almost got tickled at it. I mean, there I was praying for my boy and thanking the Lord, and my boy was still out, after all night, and my stomach wasn't interested. I know you're not supposed to be hungry at a time like that, but I was. Breakfast is about the only real meal I ever eat anyway.

So I prayed just a little longer and then I went back to the house. I did go down the hall to look in Joe Ben's room even though I knew he wasn't in there. That's when I saw that puzzle that Daddy had stayed up all night working on and that's when I knew for sure he was just as worried as I was.

I didn't cook anything, because I knew the smell would wake Daddy up and I knew he needed his sleep. I just ate some cereal and some toast. And then, after I'd cleaned up the kitchen, I went back to Joe Ben's room and looked at that puzzle some more and then I looked at his clothes and at all those pictures of him and then I sat on the edge of his bed like I used to when he was little and I cried, really quiet, though, because I didn't want to wake up Daddy.

Steve Rainey

After we got out of the dirty movie we didn't know what to do. It was about four or five, I don't recall exactly, but I do remember it was starting to get evening. It was February, so the days had started getting longer already, but we wasn't over onto the daylight savings time yet. So it was still dark, but it was clouding up and so it was kind of dark downtown on account of that and on account of the tall buildings blocking out what sun there was.

"That was pretty good," Joe Ben said.

"Yeah. Usually they don't have no story to them like that."

"Yeah. You go to them a lot?" Joe Ben asked.

"Not really," I said. "They just make me hornier than I usually am. And then I just get more pissed off than I usually do because I ain't got no one."

"I know what you mean," Joe Ben said.

We went on to the Camaro without talking. I had locked it because we was downtown, so after I got in I reached over and opened it for Joe Ben.

"You know what we ought to do?" he said as he got in.

"No. What's that?" I said.

"We ought to go to Mexico tonight. Get laid."

"Really!" I said. But then for some reason, I don't know why, I said, "I don't know, Joe Ben. It's a long way. Maybe if this was Friday night."

"Yeah," he said, after a minute. "You're right. I've got to be getting back home, anyway. I've got shit I've got to do before I leave on Monday."

After he said that then he didn't say anything for a while. He just stared out the side window next to him.

I turned on the radio and they was playing a lot of sad songs like they do both just at dark of an evening and early in the morning, right before daybreak. I guess that didn't help none. It turned full dark while we was driving around, and it commenced raining real light, more than a drizzle, but not much. I was starting to feel pretty low myself. Joe Ben still hadn't said a word and it had been a long time. I never had seen him so quiet in all the time I knew him, all the time we was growing up back home.

They was playing a real old one on the radio by Hank Williams. I'm not like a lot of old boys; a lot of boys I work with is that way: they think Hank Williams is the greatest thing since the claw hammer and they can't stand Hank Williams, Junior. That's crazy to me. Hank Williams is OK, but he's old-timey. Hank Williams, Junior, now he plays some good music. To my ears, anyway.

So they were playing this Hank Williams song, "I Saw the Light," and he was really getting into it. It sounded kind of good for old Hank Williams. I mean, it wasn't about his pet dog dying or a little girl getting run over by a car, or a poor hobo a hundred miles from nowhere on some damn train. In fact, it sort of started to cheer me up listening to it. "No more darkness, No more night." I mean, that's straight out of the Bible.

I started to say something to Joe Ben when it got through playing, but I never had a chance.

"That's just it," he said. "There ain't no light."

That just let all the air out of me. After that I really was depressed, and not over worrying about Joe Ben either.

Somehow, though, that just seemed to cheer old Joe Ben up. Little by little he started coming out of it. He started singing along with some of the songs, and he started talking to me a little bit between songs when they were selling shirts and boots and shit on the radio. And so, little by little, I started coming out of it, too.

We was back on Kirby then, I believe, over near Rice University, and Joe Ben all of a sudden shouted, "Look! Over there! A Mexican restaurant! Let's get something to eat."

I like to have wrecked that damn Camaro because he scared the shit out of me when he hollered, but I managed not to. I cut across to the turn lane and some dumb motherfucker got all hysterical at me, in a Chrysler New Yorker, and was honking his horn and shaking his fist. He come closer to wrecking his car doing all that than he done by being on the road with me. I'm a good driver. I don't cause no car wrecks.

The restaurant was crowded and they made us wait a while, but that was all right, because there was a lot of Rice students in there, they looked to me like, and a bunch of them was good-looking women. Me and Joe Ben stared at them like one of them might notice us and ask us to go out to the car with her. I mean we didn't seriously think that was going to happen, but things like that do happen. They happen all the time in those movies like we saw; that girl was so pretty, Iris was her name, Iris Hogg. I don't know how they get girls like that to do that, make movies like that. I mean she was flat beautiful. She and that old boy, her boyfriend, what was his name? I can't remember, but his buddy's name, that black kid, his was Shelby. Like Shelby County, where Memphis is, where my grandmother lived. What a job them guys got. Screwing for a living. Though, I swear to God, I don't see how they can do it like that, in front of God and everybody. She could sure give some kind of head. If I had a woman like that, she'd. . . . I'd treat her like a queen. A woman just don't know. They just don't understand.

Pretty soon the waitress came out and got us and took us to a booth way in the back, over on our right side, just near the door into the rest rooms. I was hoping we'd get to sit next to some of them pretty girls, but we never. Instead, there was two cops in the booth right in front of ours, toward the door to the restaurant. I didn't think nothing about it, until I noticed how Joe Ben was acting. He had his head down and when he looked up to talk to me he half-covered his face with his hand. I thought he was just acting the fool and then I figured out that he was already guilty, as far as he was concerned. And that's when I realized that he hadn't been kidding about taking that van, that he was really figuring on doing it.

"Hey," I said to him real low. "Cut it out! They'll throw your ass in jail before you even done anything."

Pretty soon he settled down some, but he was still squirrelly as hell.

"Come on," I said. "Let's go to the bathroom."

"I don't have to," he said.

"Just come on!" I said, about halfway pissed off.

So he got up and we went back into the bathroom and took a leak and just as we was fixing to leave I said, "This time, when we come out, you sit with your back to them, where I was sitting, and I'll sit where you was."

So when we come out I studied them cops. One was black and the other was a Mexican. Hell, they never even knew we was there.

Joe Ben settled down some after that.

I guess it was about then, too, that I started wishing I'd told Joe Ben he'd better not come on down when he called me on the telephone.

Jerome Winkleman

I didn't wake up until late. And the minute I did I knew I shouldn't have had that second six-pack last night. What the hell. If I hadn't, I wouldn't have been able to sleep, I'm pretty sure. For some reason when it gets to be about ten and I've been drinking just enough beer to know I've been drinking, but not enough to be drunk, then I know I'll be awake until I'm sobered up. But if I go ahead and drink some more, get just drunk, then I'll sleep like a baby. And the next morning I will feel like shit, too. I mean, like shit. It wouldn't be so bad if I didn't smoke them damn cigarettes; then at least my mouth wouldn't be so bad and my head wouldn't ache so much. I wonder if them guys all get together on Friday nights like that and play poker or something. They never call me, if they do. They never call me if they don't.

So I laid up there in the bed and smoked a couple of cigarettes, sort of to get the taste back right, and stared at the closet across the room. I ain't getting any younger. I guess I ain't getting too much smarter, either, or else I would be doing something else with my life besides being a cop. Especially in this town. I don't know why I can't get ahead over there. I guess if it wasn't for Kaprow, I'd be walking a beat somewhere. Which is pretty good, considering I'd be about the only cop on foot in Houston outside the station. I don't know why he even lets me ride with him. He's got enough seniority; surely he could bump me for somebody else. Maybe he likes me. I used to think that, but I know that ain't right. He don't like anybody. And it seems like the more I try to do to make him like me, the less he does.

I guess it wouldn't be so bad if we didn't have to have so much to do with that spic and that nigger. They are all the time making fun of me and Kaprow, too. I could see it about me, I guess; everybody else does. Although I don't like it. But I can't see how they can do it to Kaprow. I'll give them some credit; they don't do it all that much when Kaprow's around to hear it. Sometimes. But then, it don't seem even like when he's there he hears it. It's like it goes in one ear and right out the other. No. It's like he don't even hear it at all. Daddy was the closest to anybody I ever knew like him.

Directly I went ahead and got out of bed, took a shower, and brushed my teeth. I didn't shave for I knew I'd have to shave again that evening before I went on night shift. I put on my old Levi's and a plain red flannel shirt, like I used to wear when I was a little boy over in Orange, Texas. Then I slipped on my old cowboy boots, the ones with the heels all run down. I fixed myself a pot of coffee and then I sat there at that little kitchen table and smoked cigarettes and looked out the window at the parking lot. I swear the next apartment I get I'm going to have something better than a parking lot to look at from out of my kitchen window.

At the house I did. But Les has the house now and I've got a kitchen window to throw the pot out of onto the goddamn parking lot. Les has got the kids, too, and that no-account dog. And the good car. And what did I get out of that marriage? Divorced, I guess, is about it. And child support payments. Though I don't begrudge that. If it wasn't for that, I might not even get to see them kids. Not that they give that much of a shit, though. I've got the feeling they only go with me because Les makes them go. And because I buy them ice cream and popcorn and take them down to the zoo. I don't think they give any more of a shit about me than she does.

Well, it's natural, I guess. You can't have your cake and eat it, too.

Whatever the fuck that means.

I knew I wasn't going to see the kids, so I had pretty much the whole day to kill before I went on in for duty that night. So I wasn't in no hurry. After a while I got out of the chair and started kind of walking around, with my hands in my back pockets, and I knew it was going to be one of them long-ass lonesome days if I didn't think of something. Something that didn't cost much money, either.

It must have finally been about noon. There wasn't no sports at all on the TV. Only just golf. Since way back in September I'd spent every Saturday watching football games on the TV when I didn't have the kids, and then all of a sudden about the end of January they cut you off. You get the Pro Bowl and bang! that's it. So I was at loose ends.

I decided I would go out and shoot a little. I would take that .22 pistol I got from the glove box of that cruiser one night when I was filling in. Before they assigned me to Kaprow, when nobody wanted to ride with me, I was a utility man. They assigned me to whatever car had a man missing because he was sick or on vacation. And one night I was in this one car with Officer . . . I can't recall his name . . . There was just too many different ones. He was a sandy-headed fellow, I remember that. No, darker than that; brownish hair more than sandy, maybe. He was from Beaumont. And we stopped at this Seven-Eleven so he could use the phone to call his wife and his girlfriend and he was on that damn telephone it must have been thirty minutes or more. I was getting antsy, and I remember I reached up and opened the glove box and there was this long-barreled .22-caliber single-action Ruger revolver. Nice piece. I was messing with it when the officer came back from the phone.

"Where'd you get that?" he asked me as he got back in the car. He was one of them that liked to drive all the time. It's funny, but a lot of them is that way. When he said that, I knew the gun wasn't his. At least that's the first thing I thought. That he hadn't even known it was in the glove box.

"Oh, just something to fuck around with," I said. "Kill some time."

"You ain't supposed to have nothing but your service pistol," he said, starting up the engine and picking up his clipboard.

"I'll put it up if you want to take me back by the station," I said.

"Never mind," he said. "Just don't bring it if you ride with me again."

If we'd have known each other he wouldn't have done that. Everybody knows that half the cops on the force have got some kind of extra weapon, some kind of edge, anyway. I worried later that when his partner come back from wherever he was and found that gun gone that one or both of them old boys would be coming after me to get that Ruger back. But his partner must have got transferred or else didn't know nothing about that pistol, although that's pretty hard for me to understand. I mean, I can't believe it had just been lying in there and they didn't know nothing about it. Of course, they might have thought I was with Internal Affairs and the only thing they could do was pretend they didn't know nothing about it. That's a pretty dumb thing for me to think, too. Even though, to get caught like that with a gun you could be holding just in case you needed a throwdown, that would be pretty rough on you. But that's one of the reasons I hung onto it. Because it wasn't registered in my name and in fact there was no telling if it was even registered at all. It could have been a stolen gun. So I decided I would just keep it myself; maybe I'd need a throwdown some night myself, and if I did, then I wouldn't have to depend on someone else for it. I'd have it. Plus, I could take it with me sometimes whenever I was riding alone and when I got bored, I could go out to the marshes and shoot at rabbits or something. Might be some newts out there.

So I was just getting a box of shells out of the bedroom nightstand, where I keep my own .22 plus a .38, when the phone rang and I like to had a heart attack right then. Nobody ever calls me. I wouldn't even need a phone if it wasn't department regulations. Or the kids.

And that's who it was. It was Les, wanting to know if I could keep the kids. She had to go into work, she said, even though it was her day off, and she hated to bother me but it would cost a fortune even if she just took them to the day-care center, and she didn't have enough money to live on as it was and she hated to bother me because she knew I had night duty that night, and bullshit, bullshit, bullshit. And I said OK, what the fuck. I didn't have nothing else to do on my day off, but I could change my plans and I'd be glad to and she ought not to worry and bullshit, bullshit, bullshit.

I had stuck the Ruger in my waistband at the back, and when I left the apartment I realized it was still there. I had got my down hunting jacket out of the closet and had automatically got my billfold and keys and had just gone straight out the door to the car. It wasn't until I sat down in the front seat and felt the barrel of that thing in the crack of my ass that I remembered I even had it. It was too much trouble to go back upstairs with it. Besides, I thought maybe I'd take the kids out and teach them how to shoot. That might help us kill some time. So I put it in the glove box of my fucked-up old car and covered it up with a red shop rag in there because the glove box door was broke, and then went on out.

But then it started clouding up and sprinkling rain that afternoon and I didn't think I ought to take the kids out in it for fear they might catch cold and then I'd have to listen to all of Les's shit. Plus, I remembered whenever I was thinking about doing it that when the phone rung I put the box of cartridges down on the nightstand and then I left in such a hurry that I didn't remember to bring them with me. So even if I had wanted to take them kids shooting, I couldn't, for I didn't have the shells to do it with and I didn't have the energy anyway to go find a place to buy some.

So I picked them up at the house and we went to a movie together, some kids' movie, I don't know what it was. And then when we come out it was sure enough raining, and getting dark, too, since it was just February. So I took them home and waited for Les to get off work and then I went back to my place and cleaned up again, and shaved, and put on my uniform for duty. I watched one program on television, and then it was time to go, so I went downstairs in the rain and got in my old broken-down car and drove down to the station.

William Strunk

Why I want to be a cop—I don't know why I want to be a cop.

Some niggers are just perverse motherfuckers and I guess I'm one of them. It don't make any sense for a black man to want to be in no kind of uniform. Ruiz says it's because we got this macho thing we got to do. Like chicanos, he says. That's how come infantry companies are always crammed with blacks and chicanos, he says. Well, he's going to college and learning all that shit. You can't argue with the facts; the infantry companies *are* full of blacks and chicanos. But I always thought it was because they couldn't pass them other tests, how to be a jet pilot or how to be an officer. The square of the hypotenuse of the icicle triangle. All that bullshit that white guys get in school that we don't get because we quit school so we can fuck around on the street and be cool, learn something valuable like heroin. Shit, it's all of it. It's just all of it. It's like some of them motherfuckers on the force; they get into debt and then they got to spend all their money paying their debts so whenever they need some things or want something they ain't got the money to get it so the only thing they can do is to go into debt some more. They get into a trap that way, and most of them can't break out of it. It's a motherfucker, I know. Me and Suzie like to did that when we was first married. Thank goodness that girl had sense. I sure never had none. She the one that cut that shit out when she seen what we was doing.

Of course, Suzie's the smart one. I got my high school diploma, no thanks to anything I done, but Suzie went to college. She got her degree at Prairie View and come back here to make a schoolteacher out of herself. A good one, too, over at Wheatley. Lord knows what would of happened if it hadn't been for her. She must of been able to see into the future, is all I can say, because when me and her married I was crazy. I wouldn't have given anybody a nickel for my future. Old Man Dancey at the barbershop used to say I be dead before I hit thirty. I wasn't criminal, nothing like that. I mean by that, I never held no places up with a gun, or broke into no places and stole shit, anything like that. I took a car or two—borrowed them—when I was a teenager, but I always left them where they could find them. I didn't steal them. One reason I can't ever go to the FBI Academy; no way I could pass their lie detector test. Of course, that ain't the only reason. The big reason is I'm too black. Now some blacks are going to make it almost to the top on this police force. As long as they ain't too black. And I don't mean they have to be Uncle Toms, either. I mean they can't look like I do. I think just the way I look scare the shit out of whitey. I'll say that for Ruiz; he is the most color-blind son of a bitch I ever saw. Sometimes it pisses me off. Man acts like he don't even know I'm black.

That's the way it's supposed to be, I guess. At least according to a lot of them liberals. I don't see it that way myself. I mean, man tells me we all the same and I think he's full of shit because I can tell just by looking that ain't right. We all *similar,* the way I see it. We got differences that don't make any difference. So we busing kids back and forth, here and there, getting all mixed up together so they can see how similar they are. I could of told them that busing wouldn't work; we been busing black women into River Oaks for fifty years and they ain't integrated yet. Somebody ain't learning their lesson. Maybe it's because they make them black women put on them white uniforms. Then all them folks in River Oaks looks alike. They can't tell they're black. They think they're just white folks coming over there to clean up.

Suzie come home from school Friday evening and I was

taking me a little nap. I had all my gear squared away for Saturday night and Suzie likes to go out on Friday nights. It's OK with me as long as I can get me a little nap out on Friday evening. Then we can stay up late as she wants to and then I can sleep real late on Saturday morning. Then I'm wound back up tight enough again that I can see it through a Saturday night shift without any trouble. Though I tell you the truth, I'd rather take a whipping like my daddy used to give me with a belt than pull Saturday night duty in this town. This town is mean on Saturday night. I'd rather be in Fifth Ward; it's crazier and meaner, but I don't feel like I'm fixing to get my ass blowed away from behind like I do when I'm out with the white brothers. Of course, it's better now that I'm riding with Ruiz. I like to got ulcers all those months I was working with Kaprow. I swear that man is just like a hand grenade with the pin done pulled. I just hope I ain't closer than a hundred miles to him when he goes off. That means it had better happen while I'm on vacation in Shreveport. Because even though we ain't riding together, me and Ruiz still got right next to their zone, his and that honky Winkleman. And it's going to happen one of these nights. I swear I don't think that motherfucker getting enough pink.

I was still groggy while Suzie was crawling up there in the bed next to me after she got in from work. That woman knows better how to keep a man than any other woman I ever knew. They ain't no bullshit about that girl. She done been out there at Wheatley all day, busting her sweet black ass chasing them little hoodlums around, she don't get home until dark, and she crawls first thing up there in bed with me and just puts some moves on my ass. It's no damn wonder we been married as long as we have. Twenty years, coming up. And Lord, I love that woman. She's my lady, too.

"You still want to go boogie tonight?" I asked her.

"What I want to do tonight," she said, "is go out somewhere and eat something black, and then maybe just go to a movie."

It's funny; when she and I are fooling around, just being who we are, she talks black, and so do I. But when I hear her on the telephone to a student or one of the parents or even one of the other teachers, then she sounds like that girl that used to be the teacher on "Room 222," Denise somebody, cute, whatever her name was. I mean you can tell she's black, only she ain't talking quite black. She's talking like she's dressed up. I might not notice it so much except I do the same exact thing whenever I put that uniform on. In a way, that's good, I think. It helps you to stay on your toes. And if you watching how you talk, looking over your shoulder from time to time to make sure someone ain't fixing to off your ass, then you know you got your guard up. You know you probably going to make it through the shift.

"Barbecue?" I said. I kind of laughed, because I was halfway kidding, but I didn't know if she might really want some barbecue.

"Yeah," she said. "With pinto beans and slaw. And a sweet potato pie," she said.

"This fucking always did make you hungry, didn't it?" I said. And she raised up so quick I couldn't stop her, grabbed the pillow, and started beating me with it, laughing like a crazy woman.

"Don't you be talking your trash to me," she said. "I'm a respectable married woman. I teaches school."

I didn't know whether we was going to get out of that bed and go eat then, or not; I thought for a few minutes there that we might just stay right where we was until I had to go to work Saturday night.

But Suzie was too hungry. So we got up and got dressed and went out to eat. We went to Henry's, got some ribs and some brisket. I had me some potato salad and a couple of beers. Suzie ate like she'd been starving herself all week. Which I guess is pretty much what she does to keep her figure so nice. Got the best ass in town, I believe, even at her age. I know I can't keep my hands off it.

Then we went to a movie. I don't remember what it was. I don't like the movies all that much, even though Suzie does. She usually goes with a girlfriend when I'm at work. That's good. That way she gets to see a movie and she stays out of trouble. And I don't have to go. So I think I slept through most of the movie. Some love story, I remember that, with some black guy and some white guy best friends. Strange shit they put out these days.

We was in bed by midnight.

I slept late in the morning. I woke up because I smelled the bacon Suzie was cooking and my stomach made me get out of bed. We had breakfast together and then she cleaned the house and I sort of followed her around talking to her. We had been paying on that little old house for ten years and I had got to where I felt like it was really mine and Suzie's. I enjoyed watching her work on it just like I enjoyed working on the parts that was my responsibility.

Then in the afternoon, Suzie took off to see her sister. She said she'd be back, she wasn't going to spend the night, but she did figure she'd be late. I said it didn't matter to me none; I was going to be awake anyway, riding around listening to Ruiz tell me what he learned in school, the latest theory on how come all of us are so screwed up like we are.

I rested a while, after Suzie left. And I heard it start to rain out there and I thought, "Oh shit. There will be a few extra problems tonight." Mostly they know how to drive around here when it rains, but there are so damn many new people moving here from away, and they don't know the place yet. And because it was Saturday night, that was worse, because drunks can't drive for shit in the first place and they sure as hell can't drive when the streets are wet with a sprinkling rain.

So I called Ruiz and asked him did he want to meet me to go get some supper before we went on duty.

"Spic or soul," he asked me.

"Spic," I said. "I ate soul last night."

"All right with me," he said. "Why not meet me over at Zorba's in about an hour?"

"All right," I said. "I'll meet you there."

Zorba's don't sound Mexican, but it is. They got the best Mexican food in town, Ruiz says. And I like it, all right. It ain't okra, but it ain't bad.

So I put on my uniform and listened to the rain gently falling and then went out and cranked up that 1972 deuce and a quarter and headed on over toward town to meet Alonzo.

Willie Valdeez

. . . .

I come in about five on Saturday.
I was supposed to be off, but the dispatcher called me about four and said they was short and would I come and fill in. I had in mind to go out Saturday night, maybe over to the Cockatoo, but I didn't have my heart set on it. I didn't have no date or nothing. And I knew I'd just get drunk. I might get laid and I might not. So I decided I'd just go ahead and work. My first mistake.

So I got dressed and went on down. Some of the usual drivers were there but there was a lot of guys out sick or drunk, one. Reason Mackelroy had to call me. I drew my trip tickets and went around and gassed up and checked the cab over to make sure they'd at least halfway cleaned it out, didn't leave no ten-dollar bills lying around in there. It was raining by then, real light; you could hear it on the overhang above the gas pumps. After I got everything squared away I went back inside to the dispatch cage to sit a little and bullshit with the boys till I got my first call. I got me a cup of coffee and lit up a cigarette and sat down on the bench just across from the cage. Mackelroy was working that night. I didn't get to sit very long before my turn come up.

Mackelroy said, "Here you go, Valdeez. Got a pickup at the Cactus Motel over by the Shamrock."

"Where's he going?" I asked.

"Didn't say which one, but he's going to the airport."

"You didn't ask him?"

"He hung up on me too fast."

"Shit!"

That's the way that shift started. I mean, I know I was getting overtime, but it just seems like whenever I work extra, something happens to turn everything to shit. That was just the first fuck-up of the evening.

It turned out it was to Hobby, which wasn't so bad. Then I picked up a fare there and come back to town to the Warwick. Then I picked up a fare who wanted to go downtown. And so on. But then I had a flat tire about ten o'clock or so, and I had to call Mackelroy to send a truck out. That took until almost midnight. My first fare after that was way hell and gone out behind Hobby off of Telephone Road, down in Rats Alley, we call it. And that's where I was when I seen everything.

They was coming straight at me, chasing that van. He had his lights off and I damn near run right head-on into him. I guess that's what pissed me off, almost hitting him like that. Scared the shit out of me. So I swung that cab around and took off after him, too, along with them two cop cars. I swear we must of been doing a hundred miles an hour.

Then he spun that thing out; I don't know what kept it from turning over. I wish it had, and killed him then and there, or he had got away, one of the two. Either one would of been better for me than what did happen. After he swung that van around, it must of died on him. I was just pulling up on them all—the cops was all there—when it happened. But I seen the whole thing in the headlights of them police cars, and all them cherries, and they ain't nothing they can say will make me change my story. I don't care what that guy in the house across the way says, or that other one either, whatever it is. And I don't care what the cops says, or what the grand jury says or the chief of police or Jesus-Fucking-Christ. Because I know what I seen. I know that my word ain't worth much to them good citizens the way a cop's word is, but whether I'm a black Mexican or whether I got long hair or whether I clean my fingernails, don't none of that have nothing to do with what I saw. And I'll swear on a stack of Bibles that what I say I saw is just exactly what I did see.

I pulled up pretty close behind those cops chasing that boy in the van, but then they pulled away from me some, and so I had some catching up to do. But when you're going eighty miles an hour it don't take long to cover a few hundred yards.

Two cops in the first car were out of their vehicles, about at the end of the hood of it, when I got there. The other two cops were just stopping, just starting to get out of their car. I pulled over to the left side of Rats Alley, off near the edge of a field. There was a house back across on the far side of the van and the police and everything. You could see a light bulb hanging down inside.

The one cop, the big blond-headed one, had his gun out and so did his partner. They run up toward the van, the blond-headed guy on the driver's side. The other one went on the other side.

I seen the kid get out of the van. A big tall lanky boy. He had his hands up in the air. You could see between his fingers, the lights was so bright. There was a sunset painted on the side of the van.

The blond-headed cop reached out and grabbed the boy with his left hand and threw him down on the concrete. It had stopped misting rain by then, but the pavement was wet. The boy landed kind of sideways but rolled over on his back. Then the policeman was on him all of a sudden, all over him like white on rice. He had a knee in his chest, and his left hand was at the boy's head. I was right up where they was by this time. The boy's hands and arms was flapping around, and this cop had a handful of his long hair and he pulled him over toward me, toward the left, and his other hand, with the gun in it, come up toward the boy's head on the other side. The boy was looking right at me and he said something, I couldn't be sure, but it sounded like "peace," or "please." And then there was this gunshot; it sounded dull, like in the woods in the winter, in the rain. And the boy's hands jerked away from his head, and his legs jerked. Everything seemed to stop just then for a second, like one of those frozen shots at the end of a movie on television. Then it started right up again. The other two cops got there just then. I don't know what held them up. And one of them, which I think it was the Mexican, started yelling at me to get out of there. I didn't understand what he was talking about at first, and I couldn't move. The boy was lying there in that oily wet street with that cop still on him, and his body was twitching like a deer does when he's been shot. I hesitated for just a bit, because my legs wouldn't do what I told them to. But then I realized if I didn't get my ass out of there, those motherfuckers was probably going to do to me what they done to that kid. So I backed up a couple of steps and I was just turning around when I seen that black-headed cop come around from behind the van. He was coming up on them other two cops who were standing behind the boy and that blond-headed cop who was starting to get up off the boy by then. So I turned and ran back across into the field to my cab. And I heard one of the cops, I think it was the black-headed cop again, yelling at me to stop, to come back. But I had done figured out that I wasn't having no part of that shit, because if I stayed there, they'd kill me just the same as they murdered that boy. So I got back in that cab and took off like I had a wild hair up my ass. I was fishtailing like a son of a bitch coming out of that wet field and then when I hit the pavement on Rats Alley I got me some good traction, and I never looked back. I expected a bullet to come through the back window at any moment, or my tires to get shot out. Something. But nothing happened. I headed back toward town because I knew I had to tell someone and I had to do it right away while it was all fresh in my mind and them pigs was all still there standing around admiring their work.

For just a moment there I forgot who I was.

Ben Strother

Doreen and I never hardly said a word together about the boy not being in. I phoned over to the Higleys' house sometime that afternoon and talked to Madeline's mother. I never tried to hide nothing from her; I just told her the truth. She said Joe Ben had brought Madeline home early and then she had stayed up with her and Mr. Higley and watched television. They had all gone to bed about midnight. Mrs. Higley said she asked Madeline if there was anything wrong, and all Madeline said was no, that she and Joe Ben had had a disagreement and that she had decided to come in early. It was clear to Mrs. Higley that Madeline didn't want to talk about it, so she never pressed her. She just let the matter drop.

"Well," I told her. "It looks like Joe Ben was pretty upset about it."

"Law, yes," she said. "For him to stay out all night."

"And most of the next day, too, so far," I added.

So we talked a couple more minutes and then I said I'd better go, leave the phone lines open, and I hung up.

Doreen was in the hall listening to me. I never told her I was going to call. I wasn't trying to keep it from her, though.

She never said a word to me then. She knew from what she heard me say that the Higleys didn't know anything, and that at least Madeline was OK. The two of them hadn't been killed by one of them crazy yankees, going around with a pistol and a flashlight, poking his nose into parked cars.

I tried to take a little nap Saturday evening, but I don't think I ever even dozed off. When I come out of the bedroom, Doreen was sitting in the living room. It was starting to get dark. It was cloudy and cold. She had been working on her needlepoint of "Jesus Saves," with all kinds of little flowers and leaves, but she had quit and turned the light off next to her, and she was just sitting there in the gloom. I could see from the doorway she was crying. You live with someone for so many years and you can tell the tiniest little change by just barely looking. I went over to her and sat on the arm of her chair and put my arm around her and hugged her to me real tight. She started crying sure enough then.

"He's just a baby," she said, over and over again. And though I knew in one way she was wrong, that he was not a baby, in another way I knew what she was talking about. Seventeen is just getting your breath real good. We sat there together like that for a while, catching our breath, saving up strength for what was coming, I guess.

After a while I said, "You think I ought to call Sheriff Wilson?"

"Yes," she said. "I'm afraid so. Don't you?"

"Yes," I said. "I do."

So I went into the hall and called Sheriff Wilson and told him the boy had gone out the night before with Madeline and he'd taken her home early and then he hadn't come in at all and here it was, late Saturday evening. He had a few questions to ask me, but not many because he already knew most of what he needed from when the boy had got in trouble that time. He told me not to worry, but he said he knew I would anyway. He said he figured everything would be all right. I don't think he believed any of that what he was saying, but that he felt like he ought to say it anyway. I appreciated it, although I didn't really listen to him. I mean, the only reason I even called him was to be sure the law knew Joe Ben was gone so they could help get his body back to me. Because by that time, I'd given the boy up for dead anyway, if you want to know the truth.

Then I went back out to the end of the hall and stood there looking at Doreen a little while. She looked up at me at first, but then she looked back down at her lap, at that "Jesus Saves" needlepoint she'd been working on. I wanted to say something comforting to her, but I couldn't think of a thing that struck me as even halfway comforting, so I never said nothing. Instead I went back down the hall to the boy's room and went to work on that puzzle again. I hate them things. I remember I avoided looking at the pictures of him up on the wall, like it was too soon, or like I'd be invading his privacy somehow. I had figured out by then how I knew it was serious this time; because I never got angry at him for staying out. I was just real sad. I didn't get angry until later, after it was all done with, and I was forced to admit that I'd been wrong about a lot of things about this country and about the people in it, the people who run it and the other people, like me, who pay for it.

Madeline Higley

. . . .

It wasn't until Sunday afternoon that Wiley Brown called and told me where he and Joe Ben had gone Friday after Joe Ben got so mad at me and took me home. They'd called that awful Steve Rainey and then drove down to Houston. That's just like Joe Ben to do something dumb like get in a car with Wiley Brown and drive to the meanest town in the United States on a Friday night. They were probably drunk, too.

Mama told me that Mr. Strother called the house on Saturday and told her that Joe Ben never came in. She told him I was in early. She didn't ask me why I was, but she waited very quietly for me to say something. I didn't want to because I felt guilty, I know that. Faced with that situation, and the way he was being about it, I didn't do what he wanted. Well, you would think that that would mean that then I wouldn't have to feel bad. But no, that's not the way it works. Instead, I did what I was supposed to do, I was a good girl, and so he didn't come home when he was supposed to. He showed me. They teach you all these rules about how you're supposed to act, what you're supposed to do, and then something comes up and you find out the rules were all wrong about you and your situation. You can't win, I'm beginning to think. Maybe Daddy's right. He says all you get to do is play.

I didn't tell her everything, though. I just told her we'd had an argument and I'd gotten so angry that we just decided I'd better go home. I only told the truth. I mean, everything I told was the truth, mostly. I just didn't tell everything. She waited some more, then. I knew she thought she'd get everything out of me. I didn't say anything else, though, so finally she said, "Did anything happen?"

"Yes," I said. "We had a fight, that's what happened." I know that's not what she meant but I decided not only was I not going to tell her anything, I was going to make it hard on her, too, for interrogating me like I was a prisoner over at Sheriff Wilson's jail.

She began to worry her hands together, her thumbs going over and over each other about a mile a minute. I knew she was really upset then; she only does that when World War III is just about to start over in China or when the president has just been shot. For a minute I felt kind of bad about what I was doing to her. You would of thought that with Joe Ben gone, out all night like that, and the fight we'd had, like I'd caused him to stay out, that I might be prepared to be a little more charitable to people, especially even my own mother. But I didn't. I wasn't. At least not right away.

"I'm worried about him," Mama said.

Well, that's what did it, the minute she said that, something just swept all over me, like a big wave coming in down there at Galveston, and I felt the most terrible, saddest pain in my heart I'd ever felt.

"Me too," I said. "And I feel so awful about everything," and before I even finished the sentence I was crying and Mama was holding me just like I was a little baby again. "Me too, me too, me too," I kept saying, over and over and over again.

So I did feel bad.

But I didn't tell her why Joe Ben and I had the fight. And then, on Sunday afternoon after Wiley Brown called, I didn't say anything about that. Instead, I asked Mama if I could use her car and she said yes and so I took it and drove over to Wiley Brown's house. He told me everything. How Joe Ben found him at the Dairy Queen and how they went riding and drank a few beers and then how they called Steve Rainey. I know it isn't right, but somehow I keep making him the cause of everything. Of course, he isn't blameless, but then neither am I. Neither is anybody, I guess. Then Wiley told how he had to come back to go to work.

"I tried to get Joe Ben to come with me, but he wouldn't do it."

I nodded my head.

"You know how he is when he gets something in his mind."

I nodded again, and I looked real close at Wiley's face to see if Joe Ben might have told him anything about what happened between us. But if Joe Ben told him anything, Wiley sure knew how to keep a straight face about it. Boys tell everything, though. Of course, they haven't got anything to lose.

"Yes, I know," I said.

So we talked some more, and it was all very serious, like on TV, and finally I had to go or otherwise I'd be late for supper and to go to church. So I finally asked Wiley what I really wanted to know.

"Y'all didn't see any girls down there, did you?"

He looked real surprised, just as though he didn't know that could possibly be on my mind. Boys.

"Naw," he said. "We never seen no girls."

So I got my wrap and got ready to leave and Wiley came to the door with me and just as I was fixing to leave he said the strangest thing, what I thought at the time. He said, "You think he's going to be all right?"

And I got to thinking later: I should have been asking him that question instead of him me.

Doreen Strother

* * * * * * * * * * * * * * * * * * *

I finally asked Daddy if maybe we shouldn't call the sheriff. He said it out loud, though. What I said was, "He's just a baby." I said it several times until he finally understood me. He usually does, if I'm patient long enough.

"You think I ought to call Sheriff Wilson?" he finally said.

"Yes," I said. "I'm afraid so."

So he called Sheriff Wilson on the telephone and told him everything, how Joe Ben had gone out on a date and how he'd taken the girl home early. "Madeline?" the sheriff had asked him. "That's right," Daddy said. Then the sheriff got some more information from Daddy and after that they hung up the phone.

I was in the living room while he called, working on my petit point. I could hear everything clearly, though. I could almost hear Sheriff Wilson. I could hear his voice coming from the receiver, tiny. I just kept working, although some of the time I was doing it just by feel because I couldn't see.

When I was a little girl in Corsicana, life seemed so simple. Even though I had no mama or daddy, I never felt as if things were harsh, that God had singled me out, for example, to punish. They died when I was so little, my parents, I didn't remember them anyway. They had the polio, Grandma said, one summer in August, and they were gone before September was. I must of been only two or three at the time. I have that; all those dates, somewhere, but for some reason no matter how many times I look them up, still I forget them. Sometimes I think I remember the funerals, but I'm not sure. I may be making them up from what Grandma told me and from all the funerals I've been to since. Although they say experiences like that can stick in a child's memory all her life, they're so intense. But Grandma was my mom. And Grandpa. That's funny, he was still my grandpa, anyway, even though she wasn't my grandma.

She taught me everything. She taught me how to sew, do this fancy work; how to clean house and how to cook, too. She knew how to do anything. Not like women of today, and girls. They just buy a TV dinner and put it in the oven. They can do that all right if the directions are on it in big print. Not my grandma. She cooked everything from scratch. And I never knew a woman could fry chicken like her. I've been trying to learn how to do it right for over forty years, since I was little, and I still can't do it like she could. That crust on the chicken would be crackling and light. It wouldn't be greasy or soggy. Of course, she always used fresh chickens, killed right, so there never was that blood near the bone like you get when you buy a frozen fryer. And seasoned just right, too. Salt and what have you.

Grandpa hardly ever sat down to an evening meal that he didn't go outside first and pick some of them little round peppers off one of them bushes. He'd save them up for in the wintertime. They were so hot that if you cut one in half and let any of the juice get on your hand it could blister you. He ate them things like candy. He especially liked them with his chicken fried steak. My Ben don't like chicken fried steak quite so much. I think he just got burned-out on it. He does like those pork chops with mushroom soup, though, like I fix. He thinks I make that mushroom gravy, he calls it. He never asked, so I never told him it was Campbell's.

We lived in that old house all the years I was growing up. It was white clapboard, like the olden times, and it had a sitting room in front and then a little dining room that was really just the back end of the living room. Then the kitchen was in the back. My bedroom was in the front on the right, across the hall from the living room. That's where I slept when I was first going out with Ben, until I finally married him. Grandpa and Grandma had the bedroom in the back, past the bathroom.

I never remembered sleeping much of anywhere except in that bedroom until I married Daddy and then after a few months we moved down here. On the senior trip to Bandera we all slept in those horrible rooms at that guest ranch. I was so homesick. And I was homesick, too, when I first married and we moved from Grandma's into that trailer house there in Corsicana. They call them mobile homes now. I was homesick and I was frightened, too, about being with a man. Grandma had told me it was my responsibility, my duty as a wife, and that was about all I knew about it. I'm still learning things from the *Ladies' Home Journal* I never heard of before. Some of that stuff they make up; either that or there's something wrong with me.

We never had nothing for years, me and Daddy. He worked so hard to try to get something together so he could own his own business, and he did, too, for a little bit right after the war. But then times got hard here, and we was on such a thin margin, and he finally lost it. He was in farm machinery and light implements then. But this just wasn't the place for it, and he couldn't compete against the prices in Waco or in Austin. So he lost the business and then he did construction work for a while until he got the job in the hardware store downtown. It was about then Joe Ben was born. I thought our lives were just complete, then. I thought I had finally got to experience the kind of bliss the Bible speaks of. The boy was so sweet and so beautiful. Daddy was happy doing the work he was doing. I was . . . complete, I guess. That's when the store was still downtown. Then the flood came; Joe Ben must of been about five that spring, just about Easter time. We were lucky, me and Daddy. The house was never touched, we were up so high. It was just like the Lord had passed us by on purpose in order to preserve our happiness. All the time I was so afraid something was going to happen to take it all away from me, and then even the flood missed us. I grieved for my mother then, when the boy came, for the first time. Because then I realized all the joy she'd been deprived of when the Lord took her away. Grandma always said, "The Lord knows how much we can bear and the Lord never asks us to carry more of a load than He knows we can handle."

The hardware store was lost in the flood, though. Daddy was out of work for a while, but then he was hired on like the others to help build the new place there where they built that shopping center. It's the same hardware store that Sheriff Wilson worked in right after the war. That was before we knew him, though. I guess before much of anyone did.

And all the time I guess the Lord was just conditioning me, so to speak, for the great burden He was going to ask me to bear. For I can think of no burden greater than the one He Himself bore. He so loved the world that He gave His only begotten Son that we might have everlasting life. And I can understand now how great such a love as that really is. Because it surely is a love beyond my understanding.

So I sat on in the chair there in the living room, working on my petit point, and I could hardly see at all. I'd done "Jesus" and I was just starting on "Saves." I didn't have the light on beside me because I didn't want Daddy to see I'd been crying, and the room was commencing to get so gloomy that I could just barely see what I was doing: that and the tears.

Daddy came out of the hall after he was through talking to Sheriff Wilson and stood there a moment looking at me. I didn't look up and he didn't speak to me. After just a little he turned and went back down the hall to the boy's room. He was back at work on the jigsaw puzzle, I knew, to have something to occupy his mind and maybe keep his thoughts from wandering. At least maybe to keep them off the boy.

Sheriff Wilson

· ·

Ben Strother called me on Saturday evening late to tell me that his boy Joe Ben had been missing for almost twenty-four hours. There's just not a whole lot you can do when somebody hasn't showed up for just twenty-four hours. You can check and see if they're dead or if there's been a report on them by the law, but that's about it. You can apprise other law enforcement agencies of the missing person. But a person just ain't missing after only twenty-four hours. It's funny, too, because it's usually a whole lot easier to catch somebody right after they've run off than it is to catch them when the trail has had time to turn cold. It's not the law that's the problem here; it's getting people to take it serious that somebody's sure enough missing after just so short a time.

So I looked at the wire and I talked to the radio man and there wasn't nothing even remotely resembling Joe Ben except the usual stuff up around Killeen and Belton, in there, with GIs. I sent out a blurb on him, just asking for an alert to his whereabouts. But them things; people don't read half of them things or pay any attention to them if they do read them. Especially on a Saturday night. There's no telling on a Saturday night. Hell, in Houston alone I'll bet there's five hundred young men like Joe Ben that have been missing at least for twenty-four hours. Some of them for years. Them boys buried under the boathouse. So I knew that was just like hollering down into a well. But I did it mostly for Ben and Doreen anyway, so I could tell them whenever I talked to them on Sunday that I'd done something.

Directly my relief man come in and them two boys that drive the car around for me in the evening and so I told them to keep an eye and an ear out for somebody matching Joe Ben and then I took my hat and headed on out toward the house.

I got to thinking about Pardee on the way home. I had to count up how many years it had been, I couldn't remember. It had been a good while, come the next April. I didn't feel the same about Joe Ben, of course. He wasn't close. He wasn't even much the same sort as Pardee. In fact, I didn't really think there was much to worry about, to tell you the truth. With Pardee, I was waiting for something to happen all the time. Just waiting for it to go off. But I could understand Ben Strother. He was worried about his boy just like I was worried about mine years ago. So I decided I would stick with him on this, right to the end, no matter what it was, how minor or anything, how bad, to sort of pay back, I guess, for just being like an observer about Pardee. I mean, maybe I could raise my hand to do something, no matter how little, to make things better for the boy. Or if not that, then to make them better for Ben and Doreen.

Joe Ben Strother

After we ate, me and Steve left Zorba's in the Camaro and made a few blocks. We thought about getting a couple of six-packs but I said no I didn't want any. If I was going to get that van out of there, I was going to have to treat the whole thing kind of like a military operation. I mean, I wasn't just fucking around taking some hubcaps for the hell of it, with only Sheriff Wilson to deal with. This was a sixteen-thousand-dollar van; it cost damn near as much as Mama and Daddy's house. Steve wanted a beer for his ownself, though, and so we stopped at this Seven-Eleven and he got him a six-pack of Texas Pride, which I don't know how he manages to drink it any damn way. He says he don't care what he drinks; he just buys the one that costs him the least to pay for. That's as good a way as any, I guess, though I swear Schlitz is a better beer than any of them others. Steve said one time he went to this party with his Aunt Bell and Buddy, and this guy where they was having the party had it start out with a beer-tasting contest, to see who could tell one beer from the next. He was some sort of professor out at the University of Houston. So he had all these glasses of different kinds of beer lined up, and everybody had to taste the beer and then write down what they thought each one of them was. There was eight of them, something like that. Anyway, Steve said the one that won the contest only got three out of the eight right. After that, he said, he found out he couldn't tell one beer from the other either.

But I didn't want no beer. I figured if I went ahead with my plan that about the only way I was going to get away with it would be to be as sober and as careful and as slow as I could be. I knew if I was drunk or careless or if they got me to going, that I was right likely to screw it all up.

So we stopped at the Seven-Eleven there and Steve got him his six-pack and then we drove around for a long time again. It was raining off and on and we was listening to the radio. I finally got him to turn off that damn country music and we was listening to some good rock music. It was getting along about midnight when I said to Steve, "You know. Maybe we ought to be going over there by that Dodge place and park for a little while and, you know, check that place out some."

"Yeah," he said. Then after a little bit he said, "Are you sure you want to go through with this?"

"I ain't no chicken," I said.

"That ain't what I asked you," he said.

I started to tell him the truth, but I thought about it some and then I said, "What the fuck. I've done said what I was going to do. I guess if I don't do it, then my word ain't worth very much."

Steve didn't have anything to say to that. He knew I was right.

So we drove on over to the Dodge place then and parked down the frontage road from it. There wasn't no other cars where we parked, but we were off between a couple of buildings so nobody couldn't see us unless they was looking for us. Steve turned the motor off but left the radio playing real low. It made me nervous, though, so directly I leaned over and switched it off. It wasn't but just a few minutes before it started getting cold in the car. Nobody passed us down the frontage road, so I said, "I'm going down there and break one of them doors and then I'll come back here and we'll see if any cops come."

Steve grunted something back at me and so I opened the door real gently and slipped out of the car and headed down toward the Dodge place. There was stores where we was and an appliance repair shop. Then there was a field, muddy as hell, where I picked me up a big rock, and then the car lot started. It was all lit up with lights, bright as day. I expected a watchman or a police dog or something to catch me and raise hell, but I sort of slipped along behind the last row of cars and nothing happened. It was cold and quiet and wet. Finally I reached the showroom building. I had that big rock I'd picked up, all muddy, and I edged alongside the showroom and up to the glass door there and I raised that rock up and slammed it as hard as I could into the door just above the handle. Nothing happened. My hand went numb but still it hurt some. I didn't wait, though; I raised that rock up and this time I put everything I had into it. The door shattered. I mean it was like the glass broke right there where I hit it and then all the pieces from the top sifted down, too, like snow, or hard rain. I lost the rock inside the showroom. I reached in right quick and turned the door handle and it opened. I couldn't believe it. And then it was just as silent as it had been moments before. So I turned and took off back down behind the last row of cars and across the field and by the stores and up the side road where Steve was parked and tore open the car door and threw myself inside. I was blowing hard.

"Everything go all right?" he asked.

I couldn't answer for a minute; I couldn't get my breath. Finally I said, "Yeah. Fine. I didn't see nothing. Didn't hear nothing."

I sat there breathing hard some more.

"Let's just sit here a while and see," I said. "There may still of been an alarm, even though I couldn't hear nothing."

"Yeah," Steve said, only he said it more like it was a question. I think he thought I was full of shit.

We sat there about an hour, and nothing happened. It was absolutely silent. It let up misting rain, but it was still wet and cold. I had got mud all over the floor of that Camaro on my side.

"Well," I said. "I think I'll get back up there and see if I can get that thing out."

"What," Steve said. "What do you want me to do?"

I had a feeling Steve wanted to get as far away from me as he could. I started to fuck with him, though. I started to suggest we'd meet up after I got the van out, but then I said to hell with it; there wasn't no need for me to give him a hard time. He wasn't doing nothing but what I asked him to do.

"Naw," I said. "I don't think it would do you any good in case somebody comes along and catches my ass."

He nodded.

So I reached over and stuck my hand out. He took it and we shook.

"Well, with any kind of luck I should be home before daybreak. I'll ditch that thing; get me some sleep. Then Monday morning bright and early I'll be gone on my way to Paris Island or San Diego, one. So I guess I'll see you. Maybe some spring."

"Yeah," Steve said. "I sure hope so."

I got out of the car and headed back by them stores and across the field and behind them cars. I looked back down where I'd come from and I saw Steve pulling out of that side road with his lights off and heading away down the frontage road. I was all alone then; I had gone too far to turn back. For just a second I wanted to run after him, yell at him to stop and wait for me. Didn't nobody but him know what I'd planned to do anyway, and I already knew he wished I wouldn't do it.

But then he was gone, and it was too late. It was silent and cold and I was all by myself.

So I went up them steps to the door and pushed it open with my foot and went inside. I could hear the door hit that big rock that I'd broke the window light out with. The glass on the showroom floor stuck in the mud on my shoe bottoms and I stopped and scraped the soles clean on the edge of a desk sitting up there against the show window. Then I got the key from my pocket and went and got up into the van.

Down the ramp.

First across the window ledge, then down the ramp.

Still no noise but what noise I make, breaking glass and scraping metal. Hope the tires hold; can't see to see. Gone now. Steve and me, too. Wonder what Madeline would think, or Mama, either one, to watch me driving this. Why it seems a fool thing to do and right to do at the same time I cannot know.

I only know I said. A chain ahead across the exit. No time to lose it now; through the chain, like in a cop show. It explodes away from the front of the van just beneath me, near my knees. The radio. No. I'd better listen for those other sounds that will let me know they're after me. Will they? I cannot see how they can avoid it. And yet no sirens, no alarms; only the still black night. And cold. Out to the frontage road then where? I've got to get back on that Loop 610 and find my way back north, northwest to head for home. Some license plates? These will do tonight. Who will know till Monday morning? And yet they do not come. After all the noise. . . . I see, there. The sign that points: 610 East. That will do it. It will take me all around, back toward the road toward home. Maybe by then. . . . Down the block, to my right. Is that a cop? No red lights flashing. The light red here though, forever; a thousand years. If that is a cop he'll be here in a moment and he'll have me. I'd better turn. But if it is a cop then he will see and then he'll have me still. Trapped. No way out of this one. Except to run. At least no one can say I didn't go into the marines because I was afraid. Left across the red light and up the access road to freedom. Behind me, in the mirror, I see red lights start to blink. I was right. And they see me. Well, they'll have to catch me if they want me. And so, off we go. Another, there. The other way. I'll drop off the Loop now. They can have me here too easy. Down, around, and under. Then back to where he picked me up the first time, at the light. Now two. Great. Just great. Because with two of them there'll be too many witnesses. They can't beat me up too bad. And I still won't have to go. Out this long road. Like the freeway loop itself except not so many cars. And not so wide. I wonder what Daddy's going to say? He's going to kill me. I'll turn here . . . no name. Goddamn! Like to have got that one head-on. Now three back there. Maybe I can whip this thing around and . . . not yet. Be cool. Wait. Wait. Closer. They get closer and I am almost free. He will. He'll flat kill me. Turn now! Whip this big thing around. Maybe I can get back that way. Wait! This son of. . . . Dizzy, like a tiltawhirl. Where? All the way around . . . should I try to . . . ? No.

They're here. Quit now. Don't change your mind and get things screwed. Should I get out? Yes. Stand to face them, hands above my head, fingers open, so they can see, and fear, too. The door . . . then down the step. One car here. Another just behind. A yellow one there to the side. Like a cab. What's he . . . ? Get it all settled now. Come running there, one straight on. The other to the side. Two behind. Him over there the cab. Stop. Will stop. What! Crazy! I . . . he doesn't . . . and . . . we the other hand. The gun. He'll. My hair. Son of a. . . . Help! I. . . . No. Not. This kill me.

"Police!"

The ocean roars and I was . . .

Ben Strother

Early Tuesday morning, in the dark. In the dream I saw Doreen and the boy sitting on the edge of the bed. They had their hands together in their laps, but not like they were praying. In the dream she's crying, and beneath her hands is her "Jesus Saves" needlepoint. Fine work. Then the boy begins to come apart, into pieces that look just like the puzzle on his desk against the wall. The pictures begin to melt, slide down the walls, and then the pieces of the puzzle, too. Then only Mother's there, and me invisible watching her. I awake sweating though the room is cold. I hear the hum of the alarm clock on the nightstand beside my bed, but I do not turn to look at it. If I do not go back to sleep and it is as early as I feel it is, I do not want to know the hour. It will only make me tired during the day. So I lie here on my back staring at the whirls and disappearing dots that appear to my closed eyes, on my eyelids like a moving picture screen, and wonder about the boy and God and how we'll live with this when we finally know. Me and Doreen. But that's how it is in life. You start out alone, then you take up with someone for a while. There's the two of you. But that don't last, for most anyway. One or the other dies first and then the other's left alone again. Kids in between. And the one who dies is, too, I'm afraid, though I don't know. It's hard to have a faith like Mother's that can rise above all things to God. She believes. There's a heaven out there for her somewhere. Maybe floating around on white clouds every day, with a heavenly host, a choir of angels. God himself, St. Peter. I don't know. But surely like those pictures in the hymnbook. Long white beards and flowing gowns. The shrouds they were buried in, I guess, in ancient times. My faith is weak. Gone perhaps. When I was young I wondered, then I believed, then I forgot about it all, I guess. I guess I'm back to wondering again.

And there it is. The phone.

Across from me on Doreen's nightstand, ringing now, low and muted with the dial turned down soft, but harsh and jangling in the cold morning dark. Mother finally wakes up enough to answer it. Turns on a light. I see the look on her face when she turns back to face me. The telephone melts from her hand, drips slowly down her arm. The cord runs through her finger and her thumb at the branch in her hand. I hear a tiny voice tapping out a message from the covers of the bed. I reach across, pick up the phone, speak.

"Hello."

"This is the office of the Houston medical examiner. Is this Ben Strother?"

So this is it.

"Yes."

"Your son has been shot by a city policeman," the voice says.

I cannot speak. I cannot hear. My throat constricts, my temples pound, my heart is going to break.

"Is he dead?" I ask.

"Yes," the voice answers, distant, cold, thin.

He speaks some more, words I do not hear, and then he hangs up. There is a click, a pause, and then the buzz of silence.

I have been informed.

Doreen Strother

. . . .

The body didn't get back until real late Tuesday night. Daddy called the McKee Funeral Home out on the highway and Mr. McKee himself took his hearse down to Houston to pick Joe Ben up. Mr. McKee I call him, though I know his daddy who ran the home when we moved here. *His* daddy started the business in the twenties but he died then just as the war was starting. The second Mr. McKee is retired now; he is older than me and Daddy. So this Mr. McKee, who's just a boy in his thirties, who is very nice, said he himself would take the hearse and drive to Houston to get my boy. But on the way back, with my boy already in the hearse, he passed a wreck not far out of Brenham and there was this one lady hurt awfully bad and there wasn't nothing else Mr. McKee could do but to load that poor woman up and take her back to the hospital in Brenham. I don't know who I felt the worse for, for that poor lady or for my poor baby boy. I never knew if she was knocked unconscious or whether she knew she was riding with a corpse or not. But my boy, too. Surely in death you've still got rights. I mean, I know his soul had fled the body of clay; that really he had just left that temple for a higher one. But still . . . it seemed so public, for him to be caught out like that, sharing a hearse with that poor woman injured so badly in that highway crash.

Not that I was so anxious for him to be back. I knew I had to see him, but I was afraid, too. I didn't know where he'd been shot, what he would look like. I didn't know what I would do, either, when I saw him, no matter how bad he might be disfigured, or even if he wasn't, but just seeing him, his body, empty now, him gone to the Lord. I didn't know if my faith could sustain me. I didn't know if I wanted it to sustain me.

I couldn't sleep anyway, and about eleven Mr. McKee called and told what had happened at Brenham and how he was going to get some coffee and something to eat and then come on in, and that it might be two or three in the morning before he got here. He told us we might as well get some sleep, that we was going to need it, but we never, much. There wasn't hardly no one that had visited us yet, because didn't anybody know about it except Reverend White and Madeline and her folks. They had all come over earlier but then they had gone on. Reverend White had been there, too, for a while, but me and Daddy told him to go on, that there was no need to stay up. After he left, then Daddy and I just sat on the couch together and cried and held each other. At first we didn't have hardly anything to say to each other either, which seemed strange to me later because there was so many things going on in my mind about the boy and about Ben and about God and dying. After a while I got up and went and got the big family Bible and looked up in it some verses that my grandmother had marked years before when she had lost my mama and I read them and felt some comfort from them.

"Daddy," I said. "Let me read these Bible verses to you, that I remembered from Mom." He looked up at me; his head had been down in his hands and he'd been crying real quietly. And I was so startled.

He said, "No. I don't think so, Mother. I don't think so. I'm not on very good terms with God or the Bible either one right now."

I was so shocked I couldn't say anything. I knew Ben had been a lukewarm Christian, but I thought it surely was something that he'd just drifted away from, that he'd come back in time of need. And here was surely a time of need, yet he'd said no when I'd offered to read to him from the Lord's Word. He sounded like a backslider.

"What is it?" I finally asked. "What in the world?"

"He had no reason to take the boy."

I couldn't believe it.

I couldn't stand to listen to it. But I loved Daddy, too, not just the Lord. I loved them both, and I couldn't just go against one on the side of the other. I knew I was wrong if I didn't speak for the Lord, and I knew I was wrong if I didn't go with Daddy. So I was paralyzed, I couldn't think, couldn't move, couldn't speak at all, for either of them.

Finally I was able to say something: "The Lord," I said, "don't really need a reason to do anything, does he, Daddy?"

It took Ben a long time to say anything: "He was just a boy, Doreen. He was just a kid. He wasn't even a man yet, full grown. He wasn't bad. We're not bad. And the police just shot him. I can't see how they could just shoot him. There was no reason for what they done. If there wasn't then there wasn't no reason for God to let them do it. It's just a waste, Doreen. A waste. He was . . . "

But he had to quit talking then, because he broke into tears, into deep sobs that were so strong he couldn't talk. I started crying again, too, because there was a part of me, my worldly faithless part, that agreed with him. It *wasn't* fair! There *wasn't* any reason! It *was* such a waste!

Then Daddy said something, finished what he'd been trying to say, but he was racked so hard by his crying I couldn't understand it. "What?" I asked, as gently as I could. And he said it again.

"A baby," he said. "He was just a baby."

Then we both cried some more for a long time.

But later we cleared up some and I felt closer to Daddy than I'd felt in years, and we even smiled and laughed some as we began to go back through Joe Ben's life and remind each other of his birth and childhood and all the wonderful and sad things that had happened through the years. I know that's how people do. I'd seen it a dozen times before in my life, with other people, and I'd done it, too, before, when Grandma and then Grandpa passed. They were my only personal experience because I was an only child with hardly any other kin and so was

Daddy. So it was right, what we were doing, telling the whole story of the boy over again, his being born when we didn't think we could have a child, and then his coming up through the quick bright years, and then to now, to what happened on Saturday night; but we'd quit before we got to that.

Finally Mr. McKee called and said he'd arrived with the boy. I wanted to go down right away, but Mr. McKee said no, that he'd just called to let us know. He said he didn't want us to see the boy until after he'd laid him out right. I got back those same feelings I'd had earlier, then; how I wanted to see Joe Ben's body and how I was afraid of it, too, at the same time. After the longest time then, Daddy and I decided to go to bed. He didn't go work on that puzzle or anything; he just came on to bed with me like he used to when we first married years before.

I didn't sleep good and I don't guess Daddy did either for when I woke up once about daylight, I found him out on the couch in the living room, dozing. I went over and sat down on the floor beside him and looked at his face while he just barely slept. Pretty soon he opened his eyes.

"You know," I said after a while. "It isn't exactly the same as having him home, but it almost is."

"Yes," said Daddy. "At least he's here in town in care of someone who knew him, who knows us and lives with us, and cares."

"That's right," I said. And then he said what I'd been thinking, too.

He said, "At least he's not in Houston anymore, in the morgue or wherever they had him."

But neither of us cried.

So Daddy came back to bed with me and we held each other close the way we used to long years before and I cried some more then, though I did so as quietly as I could because I didn't want to start Daddy up again.

Folks started coming by later that morning. The house was clean enough, though, even if Daddy and I were so red-eyed and tired. People can be so thoughtful. Mostly they were from the church, but there was some others, too. Daddy's boss at the hardware, Mr. and Mrs. Higley and Madeline, of course. Sheriff Wilson and Mrs. Wilson, his wife that runs the cafe downtown across from the courthouse. I remember when his first wife died, though Ben and I never knew them well enough even to go to her funeral. That was years and years.

Ben and Sheriff Wilson went back in our bedroom to talk a little. For a minute I thought they was going to go right in Joe Ben's bedroom, and I hoped they wouldn't but I didn't really know why. They weren't gone long; before I knew it they were back out with the rest of us.

People brought food and offered to do laundry and clean the kitchen and everything. Every time I see that happen I decide the Lord was right about people: they're better than we usually think they are. I don't remember where that is in the Bible, though I'm pretty sure that's what it says. Mrs. Trawick brought a big turkey; Miss Standish brought some bread she'd baked; Mrs. Standish brought a great giant casserole that she'd covered with foil. "Put that in the icebox," she said. "Eat it before Saturday though. Just warm it up to 350 degrees for about an hour." I can't remember everything. Thank goodness Janelle was there, from the church. She wrote everything down for later, to send cards to everybody. People can be so thoughtful.

That Wednesday afternoon late, about dusk, Mr. McKee called and said we could come and see the body. I was so afraid.

The evening was purple and pink and cold, with clouds all scattered around, when we left the house. I was so afraid. I just didn't know if it would sustain me. We went in Daddy's pickup truck. That's when he told me that Sheriff Wilson had said they'd found my car. It had been left parked back behind the Dairy Queen. It was locked, so they'd just left it there. It took a little bit for Daddy's heater to warm up that cold cab.

We didn't talk going out to the parlor. I guess we were both thinking the same thing: about the other people we'd seen in our lives lying dead like that in a casket. Painted up some, powdered. Looking different.

Mr. McKee met us just inside the door. We rang the bell, like it was his home, which it is, of course; he lives upstairs with his family. He was older than I remembered, but then I hadn't seen him in some time. He spoke so soft in the gloom of that long hallway. The house is old. The front door has an oval of glass in it with an etched design, flowers and leaves, like in olden times. The carpet was old, too, but it was beautiful still, a runner down the hall.

"Come this way, please," Mr. McKee said so soft I'm not sure Daddy ever even heard him.

Daddy and I held each other's arm, as if each of us was afraid not only for ourselves but for the other one, too. We followed Mr. McKee into a room to the right off the hall, and it was a viewing room, a little chapel. I remembered something I think my grandmother told me when I was small, something I hadn't remembered in years. It wasn't ever there in my memory as far as I knew and then all of a sudden there it was, but it was familiar to me so I knew I'd known it sometime before. My grandmother was holding me and I was just a baby, two or three years old, and we stepped into a room like that little chapel and there was a casket at the end of it just like there was at this one and I saw it and I said to my grandmother, "The piano. I want to see the piano." And she had cried and cried and I couldn't understand why that made her cry, that I wanted just to see that piano. But I guess I figured that was a good enough reason for tears. I had forgotten that memory, of it happening or of my grandmother telling it to me.

The casket was open.

I was holding Daddy's elbow pretty tight.

We walked up to the casket behind Mr. McKee and then he sort of stepped back away to let us view. There was my boy, looking so pale and so little and so thin. How he could of been a threat to any policeman I'll never know, or a threat to anyone else either, as far as that goes. His face looked so peaceful, though it did look like one of those photographs out of the forties that was really black and white but they had hand-colored. The lips and cheeks were a little too red, and the eyes were a little too dark, the lashes and the brows. There was something real wrong about his face that I couldn't figure out, though. His little hands were crossed over each other, the left over the right, because I could see his signet ring with the *S* on it.

Daddy and I both started crying again. He was holding on to my shoulder then so hard that it hurt. But I wanted it to hurt; I wanted all the pain I could feel, everywhere, inside me in my heart, and outside, too, in my body. I don't know why.

"Oh, Daddy," I said, over and over again. "It's just so awful. It just don't make any sense. Oh, Daddy."

He didn't say anything; he just cried.

We stood there a long time and then we started stirring, fixing to move back some, as if to stand there in the face of our own dead son was more than we could bear to look on for more than just a little at a time. Before we moved away, something came over me, I don't know what it was. All of a sudden I was just shot through with this terrible peace; it was terrible because I felt I shouldn't be at peace in the face of this. But all of a sudden I was, and soon after that then the terror passed, too, and I realized that I had been touched by the grace of the Lord Jesus Christ, my One True Savior. And I reached out and placed my hand on my baby's hand a moment. It was cold, lifeless. He had left that home and had gone to a high new home with God. And so I touched his face a moment, just brushed it with my fingertips, and his hair, too. I could see Mr. McKee coming up to the casket.

"Don't worry," I said to him. "I won't bother anything. I just wanted to touch him one last time." And I touched lightly his little chin and his lips, so cold, and his cheek, so thin. And then I realized what it was besides him looking so tiny, so shrunken in, that wasn't right about him, and that was his complexion: he had none of those little teenage bumps and things he'd always had and always hated so much. They'd all been covered over. So here he was in death finally rid of those things he'd hated so much in life.

I heard Daddy talking to Mr. McKee but I didn't know what it was. Mr. McKee said "the head," but when I walked up to them, they stopped.

We thanked Mr. McKee and told him what a fine job he'd

done and then we left the parlor and headed back toward home in the pickup truck. And I kept thinking about the boy and how peaceful I felt now, because now there was nothing that could be done to me by anyone anywhere that I couldn't stand. I could stand even this, the death of my son and seeing him and knowing it was true; so I could stand anything. And I closed my eyes and leaned back up against the corner of the cab, next to the window, and I remembered those lines from Romans that Mom told me she had gotten so much comfort from when my mama had died that said, "And we know that all things work together for good to them that love God, to them who are the called according to his purpose." And I knew it was true, and it did sustain me.

Ben Strother

We buried the boy then, and there were a lot of people at his funeral. I never counted them, but there were right many. My heart couldn't concentrate, though, because all I could think of was just the few moments before and then the moment when the boy was shot, when he was killed. I guess I worried about the pain he must have suffered, how long it took him to die, that kind of thing. I just hoped it was fast, hoped it was over in a second. And I kept thinking about the man who'd killed him, too. All that examiner said was "city policeman." I had a picture of a man in a uniform, but there was no face I could summon to go with it. That bothered me. It was like the way they picture the Angel of Death sometimes, in a flowing robe, carrying a scythe, only you can't see into the hood to see a face. It's all just gloom in there. So I guess instead of grieving for the boy all by itself, I was doing these other things, too, and they kept me from being one hundred percent there at the funeral. First I thought that's why I done it, so I wouldn't have to be there, that it was too painful to be a hundred percent there, so I done those other things to just get through it. But then after it was over it just kept on and kept on. I couldn't get it out of my mind. I kept going over and over in my mind how it could have happened, what it could have been.

One thing that bothered me most was something Sheriff Wilson and Mr. McKee had both told me, and that was that the boy had been shot in the head. But I could see pretty clearly he hadn't been shot in the face, in the front of his head. So I had asked Mr. McKee and Mr. McKee had said no, it was around toward the back of his head. He wasn't a pathologist, he said, he wasn't an expert in medicine, so he couldn't say with that kind of certainty just exactly at what angle the bullet entered and from what position it had to be fired. But he did know it wasn't from the front. And he was pretty sure it was up close, too. There had been considerable repair work, he had said. At the time I almost gagged when he told me. There we were, just at the body, seeing it for the first time since the boy had died. But later I could talk about it pretty objectively; later I got to where it was like I was talking about somebody I didn't even know.

Sheriff Wilson had told me that, too, the day we found out about the boy. He'd called Houston, somebody he knew on the police force down there, and he told me that day he'd learned about the wound being in the head and about the boy stealing the van they chased him in and caught him. I said I thought the punishment of death was a little strong for stealing a car and then Sheriff Wilson told me that the police said the boy had come out of the car when they finally stopped him carrying a pistol, a big revolver. That that was how come he was shot like he was.

"Do you own a pistol?" Sheriff Wilson asked me.

"Yes," I said. "I do."

"What kind?" he asked.

"I've got a army surplus .45 automatic," I told him.

"Where is it?" he asked.

So we went into mine and Doreen's bedroom and I got the gun from the nightstand and showed it to him.

"It's loaded," I said. "I keep it that way."

I knew Joe Ben didn't have my pistol because I checked that after I knew he was in some kind of trouble. But it bothered me, anyway, the idea of Joe Ben coming at a policeman with a gun. Because he wasn't that kind of boy; he wasn't grown up enough yet that he could do that kind of thing face-to-face with someone, especially a grown man. I guess that's one of the reasons I agreed to let him join the Corps, because I thought it might help him grow up that way. I don't think a man needs to go around giving people a hard time, but I do think he should be able and willing to if the occasion arises where it's the right thing to do.

Another thing that bothered me about that, too, was that Sheriff Wilson told me the police had found a bunch of wrappers of some kind of sedative drug called a Quaalude on the boy. I said I didn't know if the boy took stuff like that or not. That he might have, the way kids were these days. But if it was a sedative, then that would calm him down, maybe make him sleep, wouldn't it?

"If he took several of them, and maybe if he had some booze, too, it could make him high, like they say," said Sheriff Wilson. "That would alter his state of consciousness enough that he would be capable of performing, or thinking he could perform, acts and functions that he normally would not or might not do."

"So it could have been the drugs?"

"It could have been."

So the days passed, and then the weeks.

The first cold rain was the hardest for me; to know he was lying out there in that gray casket all alone. It was just about more than I could bear.

The months passed, too, though, and the weather got warm again and then it got hot. All of a sudden I woke up one morning and it was fine.

The birds were raising a racket out in the backyard and it was already starting to get hot even though it was still only seven o'clock. I had dreamed about the boy again.

I sat on the edge of the bed and woke up a little.

Doreen was already up. I could hear the radio playing down the hall from the kitchen.

It was Sunday and I didn't have to go to work.

I thought, Doreen and I will just go out on a picnic today. That would be good for both of us. We'll go out to the lake and maybe even rent a boat out there and go fishing. They ought to be biting.

So I bathed and got dressed and went to tell Doreen.

But when I got to the kitchen my heart fell and my whole day was ruined, all my plans dashed. For she was sitting at the kitchen table and she had a picture of the boy there on the table before her and her "Jesus Saves" fine work that she'd been working on when he died and it was like she had tried to fix that needlepoint to that picture frame somehow, with pins and glue. But it hadn't worked too good, I could see that right away, and she had given up on it, because she had her arms crossed down on the table and her forehead was resting down on her arms and she was crying again just like she'd been doing off and on since she first found out about Joe Ben, all that time before.

So the next morning I went to work as usual but then about nine-thirty I took a break. I went out and got in my pickup truck and drove home. Doreen was busy cleaning the house, which I was glad to see, but she had that faraway, dreamy kind of look on her face anyway. I knew where her mind was, where her heart was. She was surprised to see me because I hardly ever come home like that during the day, not even for lunch. Even so, it took her a while before she thought to speak.

"Is there anything wrong?" she asked me.

"No. I just need to tend to some business," I said.

So she went back to her housework. She had the vacuum out, but she wasn't using it; she was dusting everything off first with her rag and furniture polish. I went on back to our bedroom and I closed the door behind me because there wasn't any need for her to know what I was doing until she had to. I mean it wasn't going to do anybody any good; it wasn't going to bring back the boy. I just wanted to know, that's all.

I called the Houston Police Department.

It took me a long time finally to get through to who I wanted, but finally I found out that the names of the two detectives who had investigated the shooting of my boy were Detective Sanborn and Detective Gates, so then I asked if I could speak to one or the other of them. Then I had to wait some more while they checked to see if they were there.

Finally this gravelly voice came on the phone. "Sanborn here. Homicide."

I felt like I was back in the service then. Somehow something like that can happen and years suddenly drop away and there you are a private again, and everybody you see, everybody you look at, outranks you. You are worse off than a little kid, then, because you're not a little kid, you've already been through all that, but you're being sent through it all again anyway.

"This is Ben Strother," I told him. "I'm calling long distance."

At first he couldn't remember, or said he couldn't remember, my boy's case. I asked him if that sort of thing happened that often, that they all ran together, or were they just not important enough to give a second thought to. Because I was over feeling like a private by then.

He stumbled around some and then I said, "I'd like to come to Houston to see you and Mr. Gates about my boy's case."

"Well. I. . . . I don't know. Awfully busy. I . . . "

"When would be a good time to make an appointment with you?"

"I. . . . Just a moment."

Then the line went quiet, because he put me on hold. Directly he was back. He said, "How about Friday at 1:00 P.M.?"

"That's fine," I said. "What room?"

I had vacation coming and I figured that was as good a way to spend it as any.

The Two Detectives

* *

Gates:

He came to the office Friday just after lunch. Sanborn told me Monday he'd be here, then Sanborn was late, so when the man arrived I was the only one there to talk to him. Sanborn didn't really know that much more than I did, but he had talked to him at least on the telephone, knew his voice.

He was a big man, Mr. Strother, as big as me. He must have weighed a good 220 pounds, was about six foot two, dark hair, thinning, graying a little at the temples. Big hands. Obviously a man used to working. His manner was deliberate, calm, unyielding. I was impressed by him. He struck me as the kind of man who, though intelligent, never had any schooling to speak of beyond high school. A man who probably didn't achieve in life what he could have, given just slightly different circumstances. But unlike many men in the same situation, he didn't seem bitter, didn't act as if he felt cheated. He was an old-fashioned kind of guy; like my own grandmother used to say: Don't complain, don't explain. I felt bad about the whole thing.

"The grand jury has investigated this case, Mr. Strother," I told him. "And they decided not to indict Officer Kaprow."

"Kaprow. Is he the . . . ?"

"Yes, sir. He's the man. The officer who shot . . . shot the suspect."

"Then that means . . . ?"

"Yes?" I said, after a few seconds of silence.

"That means that it's all over. That there's nothing left I can do. Can find out."

"I'll be glad to show you what I've got," I told him. "What I can. Some things I can't show you. Regulations."

"Yes," he said. "I understand. I can see that."

Just then Sanborn came in. I introduced him to Mr. Strother, and he went to a chair across the room by the window. He turned the chair around and straddled it, looking back at us with real intensity. It was hot in the office, and Mr. Strother had on a suit and a white shirt and a tie. His collar was already soaked through, and there were tiny beads of sweat on his forehead. He didn't seem uncomfortable, though, and he never wiped the sweat away. Sanborn and I both had our ties loose and our top buttons open. Both of us had our jackets off and you could see our weapons in our belt holsters toward the back. Everything looked just like you'd expect except somehow—somehow, nothing! I know how . . . Mr. Strother was the cop.

We talked a little longer, Mr. Strother and I, and then—I still don't know why he did it—just as it looked like Strother was going to give up and leave, Sanborn spoke for the first time since he'd said hello when he first came in.

"We can show you the weapon your son was in possession of at the time of his shooting," he said.

"Yes," said Mr. Strother. "Can you? I. . . . I'd like to see that."

Sanborn:

So I got up from the chair and left the office. All the way to the evidence room I kept asking myself: "What in the name of God caused you to open your mouth? He was at the end of the string; he was getting ready to leave!" And I don't know. I'm not married. I don't have any kids, at least any I know about. So I wasn't feeling that kind of compassion for the man. But I guess I was feeling something. And I didn't think what I was doing was so dangerous, so awful. I mean what could it hurt? But I know from experience it's best just to let sleeping dogs lie, especially when the department is involved like that; especially when someone is dead, like that boy.

I got the weapon and headed back to the office. It felt good in my hand. I've never really examined that, my fascination with guns. But it's definitely there. I like them, like to hold them, feel the curve of the parts in my hand, the weight. The potential.

Mr. Strother was standing by the window when I got back, over by the chair I'd been sitting in. I was carrying the gun loosely by the grip, in between my thumb and my first two fingers. There was a cardboard tag, like a price tag, tied to the trigger guard. The tag fluttered as I walked.

"Here's the weapon, Mr. Strother," I said as I closed the door behind me. He'd been looking out the window but had turned around when he heard me come in. He came toward me across the room. Ted still sat at his desk where he'd been when I first arrived. I held the gun out to Mr. Strother, holding it by the barrel in my left hand and offering it to him butt-first. He hesitated a moment. I was looking at his face. He revealed nothing. Then he went ahead and took the gun.

"Ruger," he said.

I nodded.

He turned the gun over several times, looking at it intently. He was comfortable with it.

"Have you ever seen that gun before?" Ted asked him.

"No," he said. "I've never seen it before."

"The records show that that gun was shipped to Oshman's by the Ruger Firearm Company in 1964."

"Here in Houston?"

"Yes."

He turned the revolver over a few more times and then he handed it back to me, butt-first. I appreciated the courtesy.

"Is there anything else on your mind?" Ted asked him.

"Yes," he said, very calm still, very sure of himself in the tone of his voice. "There is something else. It's been bothering me about. . . . " He paused then.

"Yes?" I said.

"About where the boy was shot. He was shot in the head."

"Yes," Ted said. "You know, twenty years ago Houston was known as the murder capital of the United States. Things settled down for a few years, but now they're heating back up again. Last year there were 461 homicides in Houston. That means someone was killed in this town on the average of once every nineteen hours. It was a record. And this year it's even worse. We've already had over a hundred more murders this year than we had at the same time last year. We've barely managed to cut the frequency down to once every fourteen hours. Washington, D.C., for a comparison, has had only about one-third the murders this year that we've had."

"Is that including murders by policemen?" Mr. Strother said quietly. I was startled. I felt the hair on my neck rise.

"I understand your anger, Mr. Strother," Ted said. He was restrained, cool. Maybe a little too much so. "But as I've told you, the grand jury has fully investigated the shooting of your son and has found no evidence to indict the officer who pulled the trigger."

Mr. Strother said nothing. I thought Ted colored just a little. He went on.

"Traffic deaths are up also; 25 percent over last year. And do you want to know why?"

Mr. Strother neither spoke nor moved.

"I'll tell you why," Ted said. "Because the city of Houston in its wisdom does not see fit to tax itself sufficiently to protect itself properly. Houston is underpoliced. There are only about three thousand policemen in this town, roughly half what a town this size needs. And those three thousand cops are underpaid, undertrained, and underdisciplined. Do you realize what it means to be an average cop on the streets in this town? Everyone you stop, everyone you talk to, is a potential serious problem. And then, when someone like your boy comes charging out of a stolen vehicle carrying a pistol like that. . . ." He pointed across to me. I was standing there in the middle of the room, holding the gun in front of me by both the barrel and the butt. ". . . is it any wonder that a policeman should take the measures necessary to protect his own life and the lives of those with him? Under the circumstances?"

"No," said Mr. Strother, but obviously with reluctance. "It isn't."

"You need to understand that all policemen are trained to shoot to kill when they feel the circumstances warrant," Ted said. His voice was almost as if he were pleading.

"Yes," said Mr. Strother. "I understand." He paused a moment. I thought he was through, ready to leave. Instead, he sat down on the chair by the window; he straddled it the same as I had done, resting his arms as I had across the top of the chair back.

"Can I see the homicide report?" he asked.

"I'm sorry," Ted said, "but I can't show that to you."

"Oh," he said.

"We've told you everything it says," Ted said.

"Yes," said Mr. Strother. "Is there anything I can see? Any kind of reports?"

"Yes," I said. Again, I don't know why. Ted looked annoyed. He didn't look at me, though. "You can see the medical examiner's autopsy report and the toxicology report."

"Toxicology?" said Mr. Strother. "You mean poisons?"

"Drugs," I said.

"Yes," said Ted, getting up and going to the current file cabinet in the corner behind the door. "To see if there were traces of drugs found in the body."

"I was told there was," said Mr. Strother. "Something called Quaaludes."

"Yes," I said. "There were wrappers found. On the body."

"Dale," Ted said from the cabinet.

"Yes?"

"I can't find those reports. Do you have any idea what . . . ?"

"I haven't seen them myself," I said. "It's just that they're standard in cases like this. SOP."

Ted shut the file drawer and turned around and faced us. He had his forearm up on top of the cabinet. "I'm sorry, Mr. Strother," he said. "I don't know where those reports are."

I felt like looking for them myself, but Ted was standing in front of the file and I had the feeling it wasn't just because he was comfortable there.

"I guess that's it, then," said Mr. Strother a few moments later.

Neither Ted nor I spoke.

"Well," Mr. Strother said, rising. "Thanks." He went toward the door. I had to move aside to let him pass. The sweat had dried some on his forehead, but it was still shiny. He moved slowly, deliberately. At the door he paused, turned back to me and said, "Thanks, Mr. Sanborn." I nodded. Then he turned to Ted just beside him there and said, "Be seeing you." Ted nodded, too; he turned around with his back to the file drawers.

"Good-bye," I said. And then he opened the door and was gone.

I don't think he could have been ten feet down the hall before Ted turned around and brought his fist violently down upon the file cabinet top. "Shit!" he said loudly.

Ben Strother

Something was off; something just wasn't right. But I couldn't put my finger on it exactly. At first I wouldn't say I thought Gates and Sanborn were lying to me; I wouldn't go quite that far. But they weren't telling me the whole truth either. I didn't know. I went on out of the building and found a drugstore with a soda fountain. I was really hot again and sweat was dripping off me. I ordered some ice tea and sat there for a long time trying to figure out what to do next. Finally I got it. If the detectives had been given copies of the medical examiner's reports, then there were likely to be some originals somewhere, and that was likely to be the medical examiner's office itself. So I finished up my tea and paid the girl and went to the pay phone and looked up the address of the medical examiner's office. It wasn't far away, so I headed out in that direction.

I finally found the right office. There was a nice young secretary there and I told her who I was and what I'd come for. She took some notes on a pad in shorthand and then she left the room for a moment and went into another office behind where we were. She came back about five minutes later and said, "Mr. Strother. I'm sorry, but those reports haven't been typed up yet. The pathologists talk into a tape recorder while . . . while they're working, and then we have to transcribe them later. We run behind because there are so many of them. We just haven't done that one yet."

I thought that was doubly strange. First, it was strange because so much time had passed since the boy's death. It had been way back in February, and now here it was, June, and they still hadn't done the report of the autopsy. And second, it was strange because how could the police—Sanford and Gates—how could they have seen copies of the reports if the reports themselves hadn't even been transcribed from the tapes yet? The answer to the first question I didn't know. I did know the answer to the second one: they couldn't have seen any copies of those reports.

The girl kept talking to me some more but I missed what she said.

"Beg pardon," I said.

"If you'll leave your name and address," she said, "and a check for fifteen dollars, I will mail you copies of the reports when we get them typed up."

"When will that be?" I asked her.

"As soon as I can get to them," she said.

Suddenly something just flew all over me. Suddenly I started to get angry. I mean, I'd been patient all day. I'd been patient since the boy died. I'd been patient for years, all my grown life. And all of a sudden it struck me that I didn't have to be patient anymore. All of a sudden, I realized that they teach you that patience is a virtue just so you won't make any waves. I never had, either. I'd been patient long enough. They took my boy, and now all I wanted was to find out how it happened, what he did, what they did. That wasn't too much to ask. And all I was getting was double-talk, the runaround. Maybe they *had* been lying to me. So I turned around and left that office.

I could hear the girl. "Mr. Strother! Mr. Strother! Do you want those copies? What's wrong? Mr. Strother!"

But I just kept walking. I didn't want to talk. I was afraid of what I'd say, how I'd say it. And it wasn't her. She didn't know. She was just doing her job.

I didn't know where I was headed. I just had to get out of there.

As I walked, another thought hit me: How could a grand jury determine that this Officer Kaprow had done nothing wrong when he killed my boy if the reports from the medical examiner had not even been typed up for them to read? Did they listen to the tapes? I doubted that, but I didn't know. That was just it. I didn't know. And I'd been asking all those people who should have been able to tell me and they either hadn't been able to or hadn't been willing to. By then, I should have known everything I wanted to, *needed* to know.

That's when I figured out where I should go next. I needed to go to the district attorney's office.

Something kept trying to intrude, kept trying to get through to me as I made my way over to the DA's office, but it couldn't get through. For some reason all I could think about was that gun Sanborn had gone and got and showed me, let me hold. I guess that was because I didn't know what Kaprow looked like, so I couldn't picture him being responsible for Joe Ben's death. Somehow I made that gun responsible. I've always liked guns, always owned one. But I was beginning to have a kind of funny feeling about them.

Leighton Burwitz

There was no question in my mind that the policemen involved in the Strother case were innocent. I was certain that if the boy was innocent the system would have revealed that. The same for the policemen, especially the officer who admitted shooting the suspect. It may be hard for citizens to understand, but it's almost always true that no one ends up accused or a suspect, a serious suspect, unless they're guilty. The system just works too well for that.

So when this Ben Strother came to see me in my office that hot Friday afternoon in June, I suppose I was a little unsympathetic to him. It seemed to me that here was another citizen, a father, unwilling to believe that his little boy could do anything wrong.

I've been with the district attorney's office for twenty-five years. That's a quarter of a century; a long time. I have processed about fifty police shooting cases in that time, presented them before grand juries. I've never seen one yet where the officer involved was not in the right; that's just not the way law enforcement works, in spite of what the television would have us believe.

"Let's look at the file, then," I said to him after we had talked a little and he'd explained to me what he'd been encountering all afternoon. I realized that things didn't sound right, but I was pretty sure it was because Mr. Strother either didn't have his facts right or because he was leaving some things out. In the law you hear so many different versions. I went into the file room and came back with all the paper. I remember being startled to see that the case had not yet gone to the grand jury. So that must have been where Mr. Strother got it screwed up.

"Wait a minute," Mr. Strother said. His voice was firm, his words measured.

"Yes?" I said. I was starting to get impatient.

"Look. Just about two hours ago two Houston policemen, homicide detectives, told me that a grand jury did hear this case. That they had found no culpability on the part of this Officer Kaprow who shot the . . . my son."

"What?" I said. "Surely you. . . . Are you absolutely sure?"

"Detectives Gates and Sanborn. Right over there at the Houston police. I had an appointment with them at 1:00 P.M. and they sat in that room and told me straight out that the case of the shooting of my son had been presented to the grand jury. That the officer had been found innocent of doing any wrong. They showed me the gun my son . . . they said my son had on him. When he came out of the van he was in."

"Had stolen."

"Had stolen."

"Something peculiar . . . ," I began.

"That's right," Mr. Strother said. "Something very peculiar going on. Somebody around here isn't telling me the truth."

I could almost see the wheels turning in Mr. Strother's head. I could also see that it wouldn't do me a bit of good to get tough with this man or to try to stall him off. He was on the trail of the truth and he wasn't going to quit until he found it. I've been around police too long; I've seen that attitude for too many years. You can tell when you're in the presence of it. I started to feel frustrated, angered by it. But then I realized that if what I thought was so—namely, that the police involved *were* in the right and Strother's boy in the wrong—if that was the truth, then what did I have to worry about? I should help this man as much as I could and then, when we discovered together beyond a doubt that the truth was what I thought it was, then we'd both be satisfied.

"Look," Mr. Strother said then. "I need to know. No one can tell me. Will. Can I find out one thing now?"

"What is it?" I asked.

"If there were any drugs or any alcohol in the boy's bloodstream at the time he . . . he died."

Then I knew I was right. This man did want to know the truth. So I picked up the phone and called the medical examiner's office. After twenty-five years, it doesn't take very long to find out almost anything I need to know. Within five minutes I had the information. What I found out surprised me; all the tests had been negative. There was no evidence of any alcohol, barbiturates, or drugs in the boy's system. He'd been clean when he was nailed. It surprised me, but it upset Mr. Strother. For the first time, he showed some sort of . . . extraordinary, I guess . . . emotion. He leapt out of his chair and began pacing the room, sweating heavily through his shirt.

"What is it?" I asked.

"That's it! I'm sure of it now!"

"What?" I asked again, impatient with the man.

"There is no way that Joe Ben Strother would have taken a gun to a policeman if he'd been sober."

"You seem awfully certain. Most parents are not so certain about what their children are like when they're not around."

"Most parents aren't forty when their first child is born, either," said Mr. Strother.

And I realized when he said that that he did look too old to be the father of a seventeen-year-old boy. He came to the edge of my desk and spread his fingers out tentlike on it next to my nameplate.

"I know if that boy was sober he wouldn't have pulled a gun on anybody."

He said this not defiantly, not defensively, but just like a fact. I could see that to him that's what it was: a simple truth. He wasn't trying to convince me or himself. He may not have been right, but he certainly was sure he was right.

I opened the file and scanned the inside cover sheet, the checklist.

"This case does come up before the grand jury soon," I said.

"When?" Mr. Strother asked.

"Next month," I said.

"Will there be any witnesses besides the police officers involved?" he asked.

I scanned the report itself then. Everything was coming back to me now, from when it first happened. This included a vague uneasiness I remembered feeling back in February when it was cold in Houston and I couldn't blame it on the heat and the humidity.

"Yes," I said. "There's a taxi driver who contacted the police after the incident who claimed to have seen it."

Mr. Strother looked a little relieved at that information, seemed to relax some.

"But he probably won't be called."

"Why not?" Mr. Strother asked, again tense against my desk. "Why won't he?"

I was feeling really uncomfortable now. "The authorities think he was. . . . He was just so far away. It was night, and it was raining. They feel like he was too far away . . ."

"Or too close," said Mr. Strother.

I didn't say anything to that.

He moved away from the desk again.

"I can't believe," he began. "First, I can't believe my son—sober—would come out of that truck, with two carloads of policemen coming right at him, and draw a gun on them." He walked about some. "And second, if he did do that, which I can't accept, then I surely can't accept that he would have done so without firing the weapon."

I'd known this was coming, but I had somehow hoped it wouldn't. I mean, like you trip and you know you're going to fall, but for just a moment you find yourself hoping that the law of gravity will break and that miraculously you'll be saved. You never are.

"I. . . . There's no other way to tell you this," I said. "The gun your boy had in his possession wasn't loaded."

Mr. Strother looked dumbfounded. I couldn't blame him, but I couldn't automatically agree that he was right in what I knew he was thinking, either. Because after twenty-five years a thing like that doesn't mean anything. I mean, stranger, far stranger things had occurred that I knew for a fact were the truth.

"Wasn't loaded?" he said.

"That's right," I said. "The gun was not loaded, according to the reports of the investigating officers."

"The gun . . . ," he began.

"Was empty," I said for him. "But he may not have known that," I added. I had a good supply of arguments ready.

"He knew," he said. "He grew up with guns. A boy like that. He knew. He would have known."

Yes, I thought but didn't say; he would have.

Mr. Strother moved away from the desk again. This time he went over to the window and leaned against the edge of it and looked outside. After what seemed like hours, he spoke.

"I think," he said, and then he said some more, but because he was turned away, I couldn't make out his words.

"What?" I said. "I couldn't hear you. The words."

He turned around to face me. He'd been crying. There were still tears in his eyes and on his cheeks; he didn't wipe them away.

"I think those policemen put that pistol beside my boy's body."

"*What?*" I said, with as much righteous indignation as I could muster.

"After they'd shot him," he said.

"Why in the name of God would they be so stupid as to put an unloaded gun on him?" I asked.

"Who knows?" Mr. Strother said. "Time. Expedience." He looked directly at me. "The certainty that such a minor item would not be construed by sympathetic investigating officers as the kind of stupidity a policeman could be guilty of but surely the kind a frightened teenaged boy could."

I was cornered. Something *was* wrong, I knew that. Something was off, improbable, highly highly unlikely. But I still was not swayed from my fundamental, my *necessary* belief that the officers were innocent.

"I'm sorry," I said. Then I added, rather stupidly, "I see what you're driving at. But I'm convinced that these officers are not guilty of any wrongdoing. And, as the law so provides, I will continue to think so until it's proven otherwise."

"I wish they'd given my son the same courtesy," Mr. Strother said quietly.

I felt like crying from the frustration. I *knew* Strother was wrong; I was *sure* of it. But not quite.

"Look," I said. "Here." I opened the file and searched out what I wanted and wrote it down on the back of one of my cards. "Take this," I said, "and see what you can find out."

"What is it?" Mr. Strother asked, coming across to my desk.

"It's the name of that taxi driver," I said. "Willie Valdeez."

Mackelroy

• • • • • • • • • • • • • • • • • • • •

I was on duty, dispatching. It was late in the afternoon, almost five o'clock, hotter and wetter than hell. I swear I'm moving out of this damn Houston one of these days in the summertime. When the phone rang I naturally assumed it was a call for a taxicab; we don't get too many other kinds, like obscene phone calls or anything. So when it wasn't a call for a cab, it took me a few seconds before I could relate to it, if you know what I mean. It took me a few seconds before I got on the right beam with the caller, this Mr. Strother.

At first I was kind of suspicious of him; I thought he was some kind of official, some kind of cop maybe or insurance guy. I never tell none of those guys nothing; they can get it from the library, as far as I'm concerned, because they ain't going to get it from me. But I listened to him a minute or two, and I took a call or two, made an assignment or two, and I realized the guy was on the level; he was the father of the kid, all right. So I told him what I knew, what Willie had told me that night and what I remembered.

Valdeez come in real late; it was cold, in February, and it had been raining off and on. He'd been on duty since about 1700. I remember because I was short that day and I needed an extra hand. About four of my regular Saturday night drivers was sick or drunk or hungover, I don't know. They were not at work, I knew that. So I called Willie; I knew if I didn't wait too late I could get him. He don't go out that much, don't have that many friends. I don't understand why, either. I mean, I do understand it, I see why, but he's a good guy. He's kind of standoffish, kind of aloof. A little too much of a hippie maybe. But the blacks won't have anything to do with him because they say he's a Mexican; the Mexicans won't have anything to do with him because they say he's a black. Makes you wonder. I thought only us white guys was guilty of that racist shit. Proves something to me, though.

So after Willie Valdeez had been out there among them for several hours—one flat tire I know of—he comes dragging back in here about two or three in the morning looking like a wet dog that somebody had been beating on. He always looks kind of bad anyway; his hair is real long, but it ain't an Afro and it ain't stringy, either. It kind of sticks out at an angle, like an old screwed up pushbroom or something. Like a fright wig, is what it is. Like a Hawaiian. He was agitated as hell, too, I remember.

"What's the problem, Willie?" I said. "This romantic taxicab life getting you down?"

"Aw, shit, Mackelroy," Willie said. "You wouldn't believe what I just seen go down."

"Oh, yeah?" I said.

"Yeah. Down in Rats Alley."

I figured it must of been one of them bloody accidents where nine teenagers get all torn up into little bitty pieces. One of those Saturday night heartbreakers you get to read about Sunday morning while you're drinking coffee and trying to nurse yourself back to health.

So I told all this to Mr. Strother. I told him everything Willie told me that night including when he said, "Mackelroy, them policemen murdered that kid."

Mr. Strother listened good; he didn't interrupt me or nothing, didn't feel like he had to be saying something every two seconds the way a lot of people do. After I got through telling him everything I knew, he was still silent.

"You still there?" I asked.

"Yes," he said.

"Look, Mr. Strother," I said. "I believed Willie Valdeez."

Ben Strother

After I'd talked to Mr. Mackelroy at the taxicab office, I felt more certain than ever that I was right. I must have called Willie Valdeez a dozen times, but nobody answered. I was afraid at first I was calling a wrong number, and that's how come I called the taxicab company then, because I thought he might be working. He wasn't, and I checked the home number I'd gotten from the Houston phone book and Mackelroy said it was the right one. So afterwards I called Willie Valdeez at home several more times but he never answered.

I went back to the lot where I'd left my car then and I drove on out the freeway back to the Holiday Inn I'd seen on the Loop when I was coming in. They had room for me there. After I checked in, I called Doreen to make sure she was OK, and then I washed up and went and ate supper at the motel restaurant. I was in bed asleep by nine o'clock.

I dreamed a lot that night, about some faceless policemen and a faceless taxicab driver and about my boy. Gates was in the dream and so was Sanborn and the guy from the DA's office, Burwitz; he was walking around waving his hand and yelling NO NO NO NO NO over and over again. That's all I remember, except one part that had the boy in the casket and Doreen crying, using her needlepoint to wipe away her tears.

I heard trucks going by all night, too, and the noise of people in the parking lot, and drunks going up and down the stairs, laughing and talking.

So in the morning I wasn't too rested. It was hotter even than the day before, and I was pretty sure I wasn't going to have any luck seeing anybody at the police department but I thought I ought to go try anyway.

The chief was a fellow named Shirley Boudreaux. He wasn't in his office, of course, and neither was the assistant chief, T. S. Hicks. I thought maybe one of them might be. So I studied the roster of names behind the glass case, metal letters in black felt, until I come across the name Santiago Cruz, Internal Affairs. I asked the lady policeman at the desk if she would check his office to see if he was in. He had been, she said, but he'd been called out on a case.

I started to wait for him to come back in, or somebody, but then I decided no, I'd better get on home. I did copy down a bunch of names though, in my little inventory spiral notebook that I use in the hardware store.

Then I headed on back out the freeway, Interstate 10, toward home.

Ben Strother's Letters

. . . .

Office of the Medical Examiner
Houston, Texas

Dear Sirs;
   Last week I was in your office in the attempt to secure the autopsy report and the toxicology report on my son who was killed by Houston policemen in February of this year. I was informed at the time of my visit that for a fee of $15.00 your office would provide me copies of these reports. My son's name was Joe Ben Strother. I would appreciate it if you would send these reports to me at the hardware store address, in my name, printed on the business card I've attached. I have attached also a personal check in the amount of $15.00.

                              Thank you,

                              Ben Strother

Assistant Chief of Police T. S. Hicks
Houston Police Department
Houston, Texas

Dear Chief Hicks;
   Last week I was in the office of the police trying to see you or Chief Boudreaux, or, if that wasn't possible, Mr. Santiago Cruz of your Internal Affairs Division. As it was a Saturday, none of

you were there. I decided I should write to you about matters on my mind, since I know the chief has much to deal with and since I am not sure, given my experiences in Houston last week, that I could expect very much from the Internal Affairs man.

Several things I learned last week in Houston have made me suspicious about the actual circumstances of the death of my son. First, Detective Gates and Detective Sanborn told me that the grand jury investigated the case and found the police officer involved innocent of any wrongdoing. I found out from the assistant district attorney, Mr. Burwitz, however, that the grand jury has not yet investigated the case, but is scheduled to next month. Second, it has been almost four months since the death of my son, and yet the autopsy and toxicology reports still have not been written up. I know there are a lot of homicides in Houston, but surely a lag time of four months in the preparation of such reports is extraordinary. Third, how did my son get the pistol that was shown to me, a pistol that the detectives told me had been shipped by the manufacturer to Oshman's store in 1964? I know the boy didn't have the money it would have taken to buy such a gun. Fourth, I do not—cannot—believe that, sober, my son would have pointed an *unloaded* pistol at police officers.

Something is not right in all of this. What I need are some answers. So far, the answers I've been getting are not helpful. They do not settle questions, they only create more questions. At present, it is my belief that the gun and the Quaalude packages were placed on my son after he had been shot by that policeman. Therefore, I respectfully ask that you see that the four officers present at the time of my son's death be given lie detector tests to see whether the stories they have told are true or not. I realize that the implications of my statements in this letter will not be looked at in a favorable light by those in the police department. But I have lost my only son and I don't think my request for these tests is too much to ask when you consider that fact.

Sincerely,

Ben Strother

Shelby Satik

When I woke up Monday morning I felt like hell to begin with. You *can* stay out too late, I found out; you *can* get amped. I already knew you could drink too much wine, but I usually manage to forget that by five in the afternoon. My throat and nose were raw. I sounded like I had some severe sinus drainage going on. I sounded like Annie Hall.

I didn't want to go to work that much, either. I knew what one of my jobs was that day and I wasn't looking forward to it.

The grand jury was meeting and I had to be there to find out what they were going to say about the dope and homosexual rumors. Stories had been circulating all over town for weeks that the mayor's chief political advisor and ally, Heywood Starkey, had been arrested by police in a roomful of seventeen-year-old boys with all their clothes off and white shit up their noses. I didn't believe it, and I didn't really care, either, if it was true or not. First, I don't give a damn what anybody does with his private parts. It's their equipment and they can use it any way they want to for all I care. Second, Heywood Starkey was too fat and too old and too ugly to have attracted a whole *roomful* of boys. Besides, I read reviews of that sociobiologist's book that say that he says homosexuals may well be doing what they're doing sexually because their genes tell them to. Most people say that they're just being unnatural. But this guy says they do what they do so they won't reproduce because it's not healthy for the species to reproduce more people who don't want to reproduce. Strikes me as something flawed in the logic there, but I'm not sure what. More important than that, though, I hoped the rumors about Heywood were false because I didn't want to see a big city-wide crackdown on the coke trade. I ain't hooked on that shit; you can't get hooked on that shit. It's too expensive. But I'd like to give it a shot. Besides, I like Heywood. And I'd hate to have to give up his company. I only see him in our official capacities, but if the rumors are true, he won't be having that particular official capacity much longer for me to see him in it.

So first I went to get something to eat after I left my place. There's a great restaurant downtown on Fannin, not far from the courthouse, and I hit it early in the morning. I ate a western omelette with enough catsup on it to make it slide down easy, and I had plenty of milk and coffee and toast and lots of water. I was ready for almost anything after that. I needed to find a place to take a dump, and that was about it. So I headed on down toward 201 Fannin. That's one place in that building where people know what they're doing, anyway, the crapper.

Another thing on my mind that morning was all the police shootings, police killings that had been going on lately in Houston. It was like all spring they'd just been happening over and over again. It all seemed to have started with the death of a chicano kid named Joe Torres. He was arrested by Houston policemen and the next thing anyone knew, he was found dead, drowned down in Buffalo Bayou. After that, it seemed like there was a regular flurry of such cases. I remembered the Strother case and, although I didn't know whether it was scheduled for grand jury attention that morning, I wanted to look into that, too, if it came up. But I wasn't sure the grand jury would even get to it; they might spend the whole day on Starkey.

In any case, I was pretty sure I'd get a story about something for either Monday or Tuesday's paper.

After I left the crapper that morning, I went around to the hallway outside the grand jury room and started asking people who they were and what they were doing there. I didn't know what Ben Strother looked like, and even though I had seen pictures of him in the paper in February, I didn't recognize Willie Valdeez. Strother was a straight-looking man, church-going type; the salt of the earth. He had on a suit, which he'd already sweat through by half-past eight that morning. He was sitting on a bench just outside the jury room. I approached him and introduced myself, asked him who he was.

"Oh, yeah," I said. "I've been following your son's case."

"Yeah?" he said, like he was surprised and pleased.

"Yeah," I said. "Look," I said, "do you mind if I ask you some questions?"

"No," he said. "Not at all. In fact, this is Willie Valdeez," he motioned to the wild-looking guy next to him. Then I flashed on it. Yeah, I remembered him.

"The taxicab driver who saw it all," I said.

"That's right," said Valdeez, sticking out his hand. His nails were dirty and there were dark stains from grease or oil on his already dark hands. His few teeth were yellow and crooked. His hair looked like he'd come straight out of the bush. His clothes were obviously not chosen to impress a cop or a jury or anyone else. He was smoking a filterless cigarette, holding it between thumb and forefinger. He had a gold ring on the little finger of that hand, his left. He looked as disreputable as Mr. Strother looked reputable. I don't remember ever seeing such a mismatched pair of allies. I shook his hand. I had a feeling just then that God was being good to me for something, some act of kindness I'd done and then forgotten, perhaps, or some chance to do evil that I had refrained from. I had an idea God was giving me a story that was going to be a big story before it was over. Just an awful lot of human interest and hard news, too, all in the same package, sitting right before me on that modified church pew.

I got my notebook out then and started writing notes in it as I talked with those two men.

"Saturday night?" I asked Valdeez.

"That's right," he said. "Down there in Rats Alley."

Pretty soon the television reporters noticed me standing in front of Ben Strother and Willie Valdeez, taking notes. They began to saunter over, sensing perhaps that I was onto something about the Heywood Starkey rumors. There was somebody there from all three of the big network affiliates.

"What's up?" asked one of the TV guys. "Starkey stuff?"

"Naw," I said. "Ben Strother. Father of that boy shot by police last winter. Willie Valdeez. Saw it all."

"Saw it all," said Valdeez. "Saw it all."

"Can I ask you a couple of questions?" said the TV reporter to the two men on the bench.

"Well," said Strother. "When Mr. Satik is . . . "

"Not at all," I said. "We can all do this together." It was OK with me if the boss saw me on the six o'clock news breaking open a big one. Or even a little one.

"Exactly what did you see?" asked the reporter then. His cameraman had switched on the lights and was standing back about eight feet or so, squinting into the viewer and twisting his lens with his left hand. The reporter had a tape recorder mike pressed forward.

"Wait!" said the cameraman. "This won't work."

"OK, where?" asked the reporter.

The cameraman looked around a moment. "Over there," he said. "Against that wall. Underneath the picture."

I couldn't have done better myself. It was a picture of George Washington.

So we all moved over there, only in the process I got shunted back by all the TV people and all of their equipment. I felt out of place and old-fashioned with nothing to show but my little notebook. TV does that same damn thing in some of the bars I frequent; when it comes on, everything else seems to go off. That's why I don't own one. Well, I own one, but I keep it in the closet.

"That better?" asked the reporter who had taken charge.

"Yeah," said his cameraman and the two others now set up to tape. The other two TV reporters were right up front, too, their mikes stuck out like that sprinkling device that priests use during the Mass.

"Mr. Valdeez, what exactly did you see?" asked the reporter again.

"OK. It was Saturday night, see. And I'd been way out off Telephone Road, where I taken a fare. Down there in Rats Alley. I was coming back in, it was late, after midnight. Here they come. Straight at me, it looked like. Two cop cars, police cars, and this van. They were chasing this van. So I turned around and took off after them, trying, you know, to help the cops."

At this Valdeez smiled a wry, bare smile.

"What do I know?" he asked, his dark eyes both innocent and injured. "I think the cops are the good guys and the van is the bad dude."

"How fast did you go?" asked one reporter.

"Over a hundred," said Willie Valdeez. "Over a hundred miles an hour."

"Then what?" asked another reporter. Mr. Strother never took his eyes off Valdeez. He had neither tape recorder nor notebook, but I could see he didn't need either one. Every word Valdeez spoke was etching itself into Strother's memory.

"Then the van spun out. Like he might of been trying to turn it around real fast, spin it on the wet pavement. But it spun all the way around, so it was headed in the same direction it had been going in, only it must of died. The police cars got there first. I was last. I pulled across the road from the van, near a field. I couldn't go too far off for fear I'd get stuck and never get out." Valdeez pulled out another Camel cigarette and lit it from the butt of the one smoldering between his fingers. When the new one was lit, he dropped the old one on the polished floor and ground it out beneath his tennis shoe.

"Do you know," asked one of the reporters, "that a witness down the road in a car claims to have seen everything and his story matches the version given by the policemen involved? Exactly?"

"Yeah," said Valdeez. "I know that shit. And the witness can say what he want, and the police can say what they want, and don't none of that change the facts of what I know I saw."

"It was the middle of the night. Pitch dark," someone prompted.

"The two police cars. Their headlights was on, plus their

cherries on top. I could see everything bright as day. Plus from the house on the far side. It had lights on, too. I could see it all." At this Valdeez appeared to stop the story.

"So what then?" asked a reporter. He sounded a little teed-off to have to do what he was being paid for.

"Like I've already told it a dozen times," said Valdeez. "The teenage kid . . . ," Valdeez nodded toward Mr. Strother. "The kid come out of the van. He had his hands up, like this. I could see light between his fingers, from the light in the house across the way. The cops had all piled out of the first car by the time I got there. The cops in the second car were just getting out. One of the first cops, a blond-headed guy, headed straight at the kid getting out of the van. The other one of these two went on the far side of the van. The blond-headed cop grabbed the boy with his hand on my side, his left, and threw the boy down on the concrete. The boy ended up on his back, and the policeman was just all on top of him, swarming. The boy was flailing around and the cop had him by the hair. Then I saw that the cop had his gun in his other hand. It come up to where I could see it. Then the boy hollered something, like it was 'peace' or 'please,' something like that, and then the cop just shot him. I mean, he just murdered that kid. The kid jerked around a lot after he shot him. Like a deer will do when you shoot him, you know.

"The other two cops come up then, and the dark-headed one come around from the other side of the van, at the back. And I was scared, because I'd seen what they done to that boy. I knew they'd do it to me in a minute if they'd do it to him, a white kid, clean and everything. So I lit out for my cab.

"Oh yeah. And one of the cops, I'm not sure which one, told me to get out of there. I think he was a Mexican. So I was just doing what I was told. Which I was glad to do it, too. But then another one of them commenced yelling at me to come back. I think that was the cop who had been around on the other side of the van. But there was no way I was going back."

There was silence when Valdeez was through speaking, deadtime those TV guys would have to cut from their tapes along with that "shit." I think it was because we all realized that Valdeez was telling the truth. He had absolutely nothing to gain from adopting the stance he had adopted, even if it were true. *Especially* if it were true. And he looked so totally unreliable. I mean, nobody who wasn't really interested in knowing the truth would have believed him for a moment. But I knew he was telling the truth. You could just sense it, as you usually can when you're used to asking people shit all the time.

And, too, Mr. Strother was right there beside him, hearing an eyewitness describe the death of his only son a scant six months before.

"The boy didn't have a gun in his hand?" Mr. Strother asked.

Valdeez shook his head emphatically no.

"A big Ruger revolver?"

"No gun," said Valdeez. "Nothing in his hands."

"Then what did you do?"

"Well. I went back finally to the cab garage, and I told Mackelroy where I'd been and what I'd seen. He told me I should call the police, but it was too late. It must have been two or three in the morning by then. So I said I had to get some sleep first. I didn't feel like going to my room, though, I was too nervous. So I just slept there in the garage, on one of them cots that Mackelroy has in the back. Then next morning I went down to the police station and told them."

"What did they say?"

"They said I was lying," Valdeez said. His cigarette was low again, so he lit another one off of it and once again ground out the old one on the floor at his feet. "But I ain't."

Then the TV guys interviewed Mr. Strother. After they were through with that, Mr. Strother and Willie Valdeez went back to their church pew outside the grand jury room and waited some more.

It was hot out in the hallway; the central air-conditioning was broken, I guess. We were all miserable by then, especially after the TV lights.

Then I saw the policemen come in, all four of them. Strunk was first, then came Ruiz, then Winkleman, and last, Kaprow. They walked in a single file, like ducks, their heads high, their head gear off and under their arms. They were all scrubbed and washed, cleaned and pressed. You could have cut your fingers on the creases in those uniforms. I looked back and forth from them to Valdeez and I thought, "There's no way those guys are going to jail."

As soon as the TV guys recognized them, they surrounded the officers, all talking at once. I knew I had to join in, but I didn't want to; I'd figured the thing out and I knew what the truth was. Unfortunately, being a reporter and a seeker after truth, I also knew I had to show my work; it wasn't enough to come up with the right answer.

But just as I joined the group, here came Leighton Burwitz, out of his air-conditioned office down the hall, and he bulled his way through the whole bunch and took charge of the four cops and ushered them right out of the heat, so to speak and in fact, and into his office. Which was enough in itself to piss you off, right there.

Leighton Burwitz

I knew they were on their way, when they were supposed to arrive. So at exactly 9:00 I left my office and sure enough, here they came, punctual as princes, down the hall past the grand jury room. I saw all the reporters then; I'd heard their racket but I figured the broken air-conditioner and the resulting heat would slow them down some; fat chance. I also saw Mr. Strother and Willie Valdeez, whom I'd decided should be called in to witness and who subsequently was. I mean, if it was really the truth I was after, he should be present and allowed to say his piece. If those two saw me they didn't indicate it. Both of them confined their attention to the four officers who marched past them toward my office. I turned around and reentered my office, leaving the door open for the police. I'd had some sympathy for Strother before; now I simply thought of him again as the necessary adversary. I did not think him dangerous. I was convinced the officers were in the right, the boy in the wrong, and I viewed this whole process as a necessary formality, something we had to go through in order to demonstrate once and for all that we were right. You can't have teenage kids running around stealing people's property like that.

I'd called the four officers in because I wanted to go over their testimony, their statements of expected testimony, before the hearing. I hadn't had a chance to do so earlier and it was standard procedure for me in such cases. Of course, even if it hadn't been, I would have made it so in this case. Usually, the resistance from civilians strikes me as token from the outset; only rarely have I even momentarily swayed from my conviction that the officer or officers involved were pure as the driven snow.

Eldon Kaprow, nicknamed Chow-Chow by his fellow officers: tall, strong-built, short blond hair—a crew cut. He was the first of the men to enter the room. They stood and waited for him to pass them. On the force for over ten years, he was immaculate that morning. They all were. They all looked like they were ready for graduation inspection from police academy. Except they were all much older than that. Kaprow wasn't the oldest, nor did he have even the most time on the force; he did have the most time in grade, however, as a sergeant. So he led the others into the office and he assumed the stance of leader.

"OK, Officer Kaprow, let's hear it." I had his statement of expected testimony on my desk, as I did the others, and I went behind my desk and sat down. I picked up Kaprow's statement and read it while he explained to me what happened.

"We'd heard the call by then, Officer Winkleman and I, and we were cruising along on Loop 610 heading toward the Gulf Freeway, keeping our eyes peeled for whatever developed. We'd gotten the word from Officers Strunk and Ruiz, who had observed the suspect sneak a red light underneath 610 near Cullen Road. The two officers were cruising along the frontage road there beneath 610. When the suspect ran the red light, Officers Strunk and Ruiz turned on their lights and began pursuit. It did not take them long to realize that the suspect was not simply drunk or high, but that—for some more serious reason—he felt it imperative to flee apprehension. The van gained access to the freeway and we saw it being pursued by the other police cruiser only moments after we had heard Officer Ruiz radio their activity. So I pulled my cruiser off the freeway to turn around and join in the pursuit. Fortunately for us, the suspect in the van also exited the freeway and we encountered him and the pursuit vehicle off the freeway. It was at this point that I pulled between the suspect and the other police vehicle. We chased the suspect at high rates of speed down Cullen Road and into that portion known as Telephone Road. We pursued him after that off of Telephone Road and down an unnamed road that is known by people who live in that area as Rats Alley. We had passed many vehicles coming toward us and some going in the same direction as we were. Once down in Rats Alley, however, we encountered only one other vehicle, a Yellow Cab driven by Willie Valdeez, a part-time employee for that company. His citizen's zeal led him to turn his vehicle around and join us in the chase, an action that hindered rather than helped our mission."

Kaprow glanced at his note pad for the first time. I looked up at him from my copy of his statement.

"The number of the Yellow Cab," he said, as if there were some important meaning I should be attuned to, "was 1640." I did not get the significance, if there even was one.

"Not too far down in Rats Alley, the suspect slowed the van suddenly and attempted to turn the van around, as if trying to head back in the direction we had been coming. It was apparently his intention to thus elude capture. Again fortunately for us, the van spun all the way around in a full 360-degree turn and the engine died."

We were getting to the nitty-gritty now. I laid the statement on my desk and leaned back in my chair so that I could watch all four men while Kaprow reported on the critical part of the action. It was here that the differences in the cab driver's story were the greatest and the most important. It was here, too, that there was no divergence at all in the statements made by the four officers.

"The suspect at this point exited from the van. I rushed forward, being the first officer on the scene and on the side closest to the suspect. Officer Winkleman performed the appropriate task of rushing to the far side of the van to apprehend any other suspects who may have been inside the vehicle. At this point we did not know, of course, how many suspects we were dealing with. It was at this point that Officers Strunk and Ruiz arrived on the scene."

Officers Strunk and Ruiz both looked up from the floor and nodded the affirmative. Officer Winkleman continued to stare at the floor. Something was off, but I couldn't put my finger on it.

"Also, the Yellow Cab, number 1640, which had joined the chase, arrived on the scene just after the second police cruiser. He parked the cab at a considerable distance from the van and our two cruisers. It took the driver—witness identified as a Willie Valdeez—some long moments before he exited his cab. The incident with the suspect was over with by the time the driver had approached close enough to see what was occurring."

Then I got it.

Officer Kaprow was no longer reciting his statement from memory; he was reading it word for word from his note pad. At first I was alarmed; but then I realized that he was simply being prudent. He was aware of the specific differences between the cab driver's statement and his and the other officers' statements, and he was simply making certain that his version would be as accurately stated as possible. I reminded myself to tell him, however, that his testimony would be stronger before the jury if he did not read that part of it but instead recited from memory as he had done the first part.

"Go on," I said. The other three officers were all staring at the floor again. Though none of them made a movement, I could tell this ordeal made them uncomfortable. I didn't blame them; they do a thankless job and then have to defend themselves. I don't know why anyone in his right mind would even want to be a cop.

"The suspect exited the van and I saw something in his right hand, although I could not be sure what it was. One of the other officers—I am not certain who it was—yelled 'Look out! He's got a gun!' So I rushed forward, my own gun drawn, to tackle the man. In the course of that action which the intent of it was to disarm the suspect, I shot him. It was not my intention to shoot the man, or to kill him; I simply acted instinctively, as I have been trained, to protect my own life and those of others when faced with such a situation."

He looked up from his note pad now.

"A suspect with a drawn pistol, approaching in a menacing fashion," he said. "I had no choice. It was self-defense."

The other officers all nodded the affirmative. Ruiz and Winkleman looked at Kaprow and then looked away. Strunk never raised his eyes.

All four men looked out of place, though they all looked impeccable in their tailored and fitted uniforms. Witnessing is the hardest job that men like that are called upon to do; they are doers, not talkers, and it is out of their character to have to substitute the one for the other.

"Men," I said. They all looked up at me. "I want you to know that I know your testimony is accurate. I know you are telling the truth. I wouldn't ordinarily even insult you by assuring you of such a thing, but as you know, we have unfriendly witnesses in the building today who will be testifying before the grand jury also." The men all looked relieved and then concerned again, in that order.

"But I wouldn't worry about it too much, if I were you. Your statements are all consistent with each other in the disputed areas and—let's face it. . . ." I got up from my chair and came around and sat up on the front of my desk. "Let's face it. The witness for the other side is a scruffy looking. . . . " I caught myself before I said anything to offend either Strunk or Ruiz. "A scruffy-looking cab driver who hasn't had a haircut in a month of Sundays. His credibility with the members of the grand jury is not going to be great. I see absolutely no reason to worry about anything."

They all stood up. Everyone except Strunk smiled at me.

"No. Stay here," I said. "The air-conditioner is broken out there." I gestured toward my humming window unit. "Just relax until you're called."

I went to the door.

"I'll be in the DA's office," I said, "if you need me."

Allan Durnier

We didn't even get to the police shooting case until after three. The whole morning was taken up with testimony on the Heywood Starkey matter. What a case of political assassination that one was. I swear to God that some people will do absolutely anything for a little bit of power, anything. So by the time we'd cleaned that matter up and had taken a break and were ready to start on the shooting case, it was fairly late in the afternoon. I was tired and hot, even though we did have some window units, and the other members of the jury were just as upset with the whole day as I was. I'm sure they thought like I did that we'd finish the first half of that police matter within an hour and be out of that place by four o'clock. We weren't counting on Mr. Strother's patience and stubbornness.

I began the proceedings in my function as foreman by pointing out to the other jury members the criminal history of the shooting victim back in his hometown. I wanted them to understand that what the police were dealing with was not just some innocent young kid.

But I didn't get three sentences out before the boy's father stood up, wanting to speak. I started not to recognize him, but there was something about him that made me realize it wouldn't do any good to ignore him; that he was prepared to stand there patiently for the rest of the night if he had to. He was really wilted looking. The big air-conditioner had been out since sometime during the night, and the hallways and restrooms and places like that were absolutely miserable. For just a second I felt kind of bad for the man; but I stopped right away. For one thing, it doesn't do a bit of good to get emotionally involved in any of the cases we're called upon to investigate accusations about, and for another, I reminded myself that if he'd of raised that boy up the right way, then he wouldn't of ever done anything to get himself shot for. Those things are the result of early training, in my opinion, or the lack of it. So I said, "Yes, what is it, Mr. Strother?"

"I don't hold with stealing hubcaps or anything else, like my boy did," he said. "And I don't hold with him taking that van, stealing that van that didn't belong to him, either. But that isn't why I'm here. If my boy sure enough came after those officers with a gun in his hand, even an unloaded gun, then I don't deny for a minute that what they did was the right thing for them to do. As hard as it is for me to say that and to accept it, I do. I'm only here because there are some things that I think ought to be looked into in this case, things that don't add up."

"Yes," I said. "I can see your concern." I could see it, too. Not for the same reasons he had, though. I glanced around at the other jurors and saw that out of the whole mess of them only a couple of them was paying any attention at all to what the man was saying. One was that woman with a nephew who would of been just about the dead boy's age. The other was that Mexican fellow, in his early middle age. I swear to God that two others of them was asleep, and the rest looked like they couldn't care less what the man was talking about, what he'd lost or nothing.

So then I told him to go ahead and say what was on his mind and he did. He cited some evidence here and there that struck me as mostly guesses or wishful thinking. Some of it may have had some basis in something, but I for one wasn't convinced. It just seemed to me a case of a man who just couldn't believe his son was really dead and that to do what he was doing might somehow magically bring him back.

It didn't take him long to have his say. When he was finished I asked the other jurors if they had any questions. The lady with the teenager raised her hand.

"Yes," I said. "Go ahead."

"How old was your boy?" she asked.

"Seventeen," said Mr. Strother.

She just shook her head and clucked her tongue. I could see where she was coming from, what she was thinking.

I said, "Is that it, then? Are there any other questions?" I halfway expected that Mexican to have something to add, but he didn't raise his hand. I waited for a few moments.

"OK," I said. "Thank you very much for your testimony, Mr. Strother. You may be excused from the courtroom now." I nodded toward the bailiff, who came toward Mr. Strother and then escorted him out of the room.

I started to go ahead and call in that Willie Valdeez guy, but I looked around at my sterling crew again and saw now that three of them were nodding off. Well, it had been a long day and it does take a lot out of you to have to listen to a lot of smut about homosexuals and dope and all that stuff.

So I said, "I'll entertain a motion to adjourn."

One of the sleepers sat straight up and said, "I move we adjourn for the day."

Someone else seconded it and so we stood adjourned.

I told the bailiff to tell Willie Valdeez in the corridor that he would not be testifying that day, that he should come back in the morning promptly at 8:00. I had already seen we weren't going to get to the policemen that day anyway, so I had sent the word at the noon lunch break for them to be dismissed until the following day. I wasn't being unfair; I had thought we'd get to Valdeez. In fact, I was being very fair. The jury simply wasn't in any condition to listen carefully to any complicated testimony. And this, after all, was a case about a shooting; we could conceivably end up indicting one or more of those officers for trial before a petit jury, although I for one doubted it. I'm not saying I had my mind made up before I heard all the evidence, because I didn't. But I did know from my experience already of more than six months as foreman of that grand jury that every other similar police shooting case we'd heard with the exception of one was clearly on the side of the police and not the victim. That was the Joe Campos Torres case. That was a pretty sticky one. We did vote to indict for trial on that one; God knows how long it will be before it is settled, too.

But this one seemed pretty clear. And the charge that the police might have planted an unloaded gun on that boy after he was shot was simply beyond my belief. I don't care how dumb anyone thinks or says a cop is, I've never met one yet that dumb. It just wasn't something one of them would think he could get away with.

So we adjourned for the day and everyone left. It took me a while to get things squared away, to make sure the transcriptions of the proceedings were secured and so on, and finally then I left, too.

If I'd known then what I was to find out later, I would have stayed gone, too; I sure as hell wouldn't have come back the next day. Or if I had come back, I would have listened more carefully to the facts and been less swayed by the appearances of things.

Live and learn.

Willie Valdeez

I ain't saying people are prejudiced or nothing; I never have felt comfortable claiming that when other people treat me like shit. Plus, the nuns done a pretty good job of tempering me so I'm usually hard enough that I can take anything they can think up to put on my ass. But I was a little pissed off that day at the grand jury. Because first they never believed a word I said about what I seen anyway. And then, when it looked to me like they thought they just couldn't get out of it, they decided I was at least responsible enough to be called in to testify before the jury. So they called me in at eight o'clock on a Monday morning, which was punishment enough by itself, but then the motherfuckers made me sit in that goddamned steam bath son of a bitch hallway from eight in the morning till four o'clock in the afternoon and never called my ass in to testify nothing. Plus, too, them fucking pigs that murdered that kid come late, waited a couple of hours in a air-conditioned office, then left by noon. I will say they did make Mr. Strother wait, too. So I guess the thing is, they wasn't prejudiced about me because of my races, but they was prejudiced on both of us because we was against the side of the police. See, even the jury is on the side of the police. A lot of people don't see that. Or if they do, they say, sure, they should be. But that's just because they're going on the idea that the police never fuck up, that they're always right. Well, I'll tell you one thing: there was only one perfect person ever on this earth and they crucified Him. So don't tell me.

Mr. Strother was just going in the building when I got there that morning. Mackelroy had told me he'd called at work when he was in town before. He never did get ahold of me. I never was exactly sure where he lived or nothing or maybe I would of gone there and talked to him or something. But the truth is, I didn't really want to see him. I mean it was his boy I seen murdered by them cops. I didn't know what kind of man he was or nothing and whether he'd ask me a whole lot of questions and shit and whether he'd cry or whether he'd believe me or not. I didn't know how he'd take me being half-black and half-Mexican either. I haven't found very many people that that don't blow their mind some kind of way. I didn't recognize him when I seen him. I mean, I had no idea what the man looked like and I didn't know what he was doing at the grand jury place. I never probably would of even noticed him if he hadn't of been looking at me like he was. Of course, a lot of people do look at me funny, because of my hair and because I don't look like I'm black or Mexican but some of both. I'm pretty much used to being stared at, especially by little kids; a lot like an albino is, I figure. But this guy wasn't looking at me like that; he was looking at me like he was trying to decide whether to say something to me or not.

When we both got inside the building and was looking for that room number and we was still together, he finally did speak.

"You here for the grand jury?" he asked.

"Right," I said. "You too?"

"That's right," he said.

We found the room then and we stood around some. I lit a cigarette. I even offered him one; he seemed like a nice enough guy. He wasn't offended by the way I look, which just a awful lot of *gringo* ofay son of a bitches can't get past, can't abide. He declined, though. And then after a few minutes, a bailiff came out and talked to both of us and asked us our names and that's when we both found out who the other one was.

So after the bailiff told us to sit down and wait, we started talking to each other, and he never pressed me too much about asking questions or anything. I was just fixing to start telling him on my own everything I seen when this reporter come over and asked us who we was and then commenced asking me all kinds of questions. The hallway was really getting filled up with people by then, a bunch of TV cameras and all kinds of shit. Then some of them come over to where we was sitting on the bench, and they got interested, and the next thing I know I'm up against the wall, motherfucker, with bright-ass lights shining in my face and microphones poking all at me, making me nervous as shit. Be on TV. They give me some shit at work, I'll tell you that.

I told the truth about what I seen.

I figured my ass was already grass with every cop in Houston, so I didn't have nothing to lose. Besides, I couldn't change my story and start lying now. Although I swear I couldn't remember so good what I seen that night as I could remember what I'd been saying about it for six months. That's the nice thing about telling the truth, though: you don't have to remember. The nuns taught me that, too.

So then Mr. Strother and I went back to the bench and sat there some more. He asked me one or two questions about details, but then he let it go. I was glad, although he certainly made it easy for me. I mean, it was like he didn't really care what I did tell him. Lots of people, when you're talking to them and you tell them something they don't want to hear, that they want it to be something else, they will flat use body english, like a guy shooting pool, to try to get what you say to be something else, whatever it is they want it to be. But he didn't do that. Of course, what I was saying was probably what he wanted to hear, as much as it could be, being it was the killing of his son we was talking about.

Then directly we quit talking together. Then we went to eat lunch when the bailiff come out and told us. That's when the pigs left and never come back. After lunch me and Mr. Strother sat there on that hard-ass bench just like we was in church and sort of halfway dozed off and on, and sweated and farted, and waited to be called.

A little after three o'clock, sometime, they called Mr. Strother in. Then after about twenty minutes or so he come back out and sat down there with me again. We waited some more and then about four o'clock the bailiff come out and I thought then I was going in but instead he told me to go on home, that I was released, that I should come back in the morning at eight o'clock again.

I swear, if Mr. Strother had not been such a decent guy, and if I hadn't of had to take every chance I could to prove I wasn't no liar, I would of told the bailiff and the whole goddamned grand jury they could stick it up their ass. I never would of come back down that same row. But under the circumstances, I didn't.

Mr. Strother and I went outside. It seemed to me like he didn't want me to go off without him, that he was worried I might not come back in the morning. But I was going to the Cockatoo for a while and I sure as hell couldn't take him or any other white dude in there with me. So I told him not to worry, and I sort of patted him on the shoulder before I realized it, and he smiled at me and said, "Thanks. See you tomorrow." And he went his way and I went mine and that was that.

The Other Witnesses

∙ ∙

Birdy Shepherd:

I seen on television where that Mexican nigger was telling what he seen them policemen do to that boy that Saturday night back whenever it was, in February sometime. So I figured I did see what I thought I seen that night and I ought to come forward and tell about it. So I did. I called the police and told them and they gave me the number of this Leighton Burwitz guy in the DA's office and so I called him. He told me where to come to, down on Fannin, and what day and everything, so I got all ready and come on down.

My wife said I ought not to do it. She was probably right, as it turned out. What I said to them suckers didn't make no difference at all to them. But I did feel better about it; I'd been kind of worrying that I had seen what I seen and didn't never say anything about it to no one. I suppose seeing that fellow on the television made me feel guilty; him, and seeing that boy's daddy standing there next to him.

The wife and I had a boy once, too, but that was many years ago. He was killed in Korea when he wasn't no older than that boy the police killed. But at least our son had a chance, he had a gun to defend himself with. This boy didn't have nothing. I know, because I seen it all.

I was watching the television late that Saturday evening, having a few beers; I don't know what it was. Some old cowboy movie, I believe. I had sort of been sleeping on and off, you know, in the chair, and then I heard this noise that startled me, woke me up, because it didn't fit in with the noise of the western movie on the television. I realized pretty quick that it was the sirens of them police cars and they were coming closer and coming closer and pretty soon I got up and went outside to look. It was cold out there and it woke me up pretty quick. Here they come, right down into Rats Alley, going a hundred miles an hour it looked like. Then the van, the one the police was chasing, it spun around in a circle, you know. It didn't turn over, but just spun around in a circle until it ended up headed back the way it had been going in the first place. Then this taxicab come up and there was two police cars already. So I moved off the front porch there, in my slippers, and went out away from the building, into the shadows beyond the light, to get me an angle so I could see. Then I seen the whole thing, pretty near, just like that nigger told it on the television.

This big tall kid come down out of the van; he was down when I cleared where I could see, and he had his hands up. I could see a policeman on my side of the van; he opened the door and looked in there. And I could see the other policemen coming up behind the big blond one. Across on the other side I seen that taxicab and that Mexican nigger coming right up into the middle of everything. Then the tall policeman with the blond hair and I think another one, too, jumped on that kid and knocked him down and shot him, just like that. Damnedest thing I ever seen. The cop on this side went back around where the others all were. And the taxicab driver jumped back in his cab and took off like a bat out of hell.

I started edging real quiet back toward my place, because I was afraid if they seen me, the cops, they'd shoot my ass, too, like they done that kid. I was going toward the side of the building so I could go in the back door. That's when I seen the cop that had been on my side of the van go back to one of the police cars and come back with that big pistol in his hand. And that's when I knowed it was time for me to make myself so scarce that couldn't none of them see me. And I did.

Jim Lambert:
   I seen that nigger lying through his teeth on TV and I just decided that goddamn it, there wasn't no equal protection under the law that made that right. It just goes to show how a self-respecting white man like that boy's father can let himself be taken in by one of them if he says what they want to hear. Because, by God, it's just like Vietnam. If we would of just gone in there and won that war, we could of. There wouldn't have been no problems. But all we done was pussyfoot here and pussyfoot there and of course then we snuck out of there like whipped dogs.
   I ain't saying the police have got a license to kill. I ain't saying that they can just shoot anybody for no reason at all. But that's just the point; it ain't the way that nigger said. It just didn't happen like that. I know, because I seen the whole thing.
   I come out of a side road down to my place and pulled onto Rats Alley just as they come by, them police cars chasing that van and that lying nigger in his yellow taxicab. I was heading in the same direction as them, going east, toward work. My shift started at 2:30 that morning, on the railroad, and I had just woke up and ate some breakfast and had me some coffee, so I was bright-eyed and bushy-tailed. I mean I was alert. I had my thermos there with me in the car, tucked between my legs.
   When I pulled up onto Rats Alley I never figured I'd see them cars and that van again; I figured they'd be long gone. But I come around a bend just a little ways down the road and there they all were, all spread out and lit up like they was having a street dance. It was kind of eerie, too, because it had been misting rain earlier and although it was not quite foggy, still, you could see the air, if you know what I mean. So them headlights lit things up clearly, but they made kind of a halo on things too. And them red lights going around on the top of the cars danced a red glow off of things. It was scary, but it was clear.
   So when I seen them up ahead, I just pulled off to the side of the road and shut off my lights, turned off my engine. Because there was no telling what was going to come down and I wanted to be out of the way but ready to help if I was needed.

I very carefully screwed the top back on my vacuum bottle and put it in the console slot there next to me. Then I reached down under the seat of that Ford Thunderbird of mine and searched around until I found my gun. I slipped it out and then took it out of the holster and then I sat there and waited. I never had shot a person with that Colt revolver of mine, but I was ready to if it turned out them police needed a hand.

They never.

That punk come down out of that van with something in his right hand, some object. Now I can't say for certain that it was a gun that boy was carrying but I can say that it surely could have been, and if I had been in them policemen's shoes I surely would have shot first and then asked questions later. I know my hand tightened up on my pistol when I seen there was something in that boy's hand. As it turned out, I was right. Because I seen where the police found he had a gun after they had shot him.

I don't say they have a license to kill, but I do say they sure as hell can't protect us if they can't protect themselves. And I seen it all, and that's by God all they done.

Allan Durnier

So after we'd finally heard the testimony of that Valdeez fellow, then we had the four policemen in before the jury. I'm telling the truth, the contrast was so great between the two sides, you didn't really have to even listen to them to see which one was most likely telling the truth and which one lying. I know I shouldn't say that, but it's the truth. Of course, I'm not talking about Mr. Strother. But he didn't seem like he was on the other side from the police; he seemed more like he was just neutral, if you get my meaning. It was Valdeez on the one side, calling those officers liars and claiming they murdered that boy in cold blood, and then the officers on the other side, calmly—and neatly and cleanly in the bargain—claiming they never did anything but their duty.

After we'd heard the testimony of we thought everybody, we debated the matter. It didn't take very long for us to decide that the shooting by Officer Kaprow had been in the line of duty and that he had acted within the limits of the law. We decided not to indict. It wasn't just the appearances; that only underscored the truth of things. It was the evidence, including the county medical examiner along with everybody else.

Then the very first of the next week along come these two new witnesses that we didn't know anything about them before, that came forward after they'd seen Valdeez and Strother and Burwitz on television. At first it was my inclination simply to say they were too late, they'd taken their hands off their checkers and their moves were over. But by then, the newspapers were having a field day and I knew that even if these new witnesses didn't change the final conclusion one bit, still, the grand jury would be tainted if we didn't allow them to come forward and tell their stories. We were about halfway suspect anyway for returning No Indictment in the Heywood Starkey case. I'm just as sure—no, more sure—there was no more merit in those accusations than there was in those made by Valdeez against Kaprow.

So there I had this Birdy Shepherd, admittedly drinking the night of the incident, whose testimony seemed to me to be designed around saying the exact opposite of what the policemen's story was; him on the one hand. And on the other hand I had this James Lambert, who turned out to be just a little on the right of Attila the Hun, politically speaking. I mean, I'm a conservative Democrat, but good Lord, that boy was *conservative*. He was still wearing a flattop. And *he* admittedly had stopped his car a good two hundred feet away from the incident, which didn't exactly make for a close-up view of the situation at two or three in the morning. But I understand why Burwitz brought them in and I know why we listened to them and I was absolutely certain that neither changed the balance of things one iota. We did our duty, though.

That was late in the month. After Birdy Shepherd and James Lambert had done their part and had left, we debated the matter again, this time for about five minutes, and we agreed that there was no compelling evidence that compelled us to consider voting to open the case. So I took a vote and we voted unanimously not to move to open. We didn't vote unanimously the first time, because there were two holdouts, but after some subtle persuasion and some back-in-the-corner trading, the two holdouts came around and then we broke for the day and I secured everything and we all went home.

It rained that day and cooled things off for about five minutes, but then it just got steamier and steamier. That was a Friday, at the end of July, and since I didn't have nothing the next day, work or jury duty either one, I got drunk after I got home, and watched a "Rockford Files" rerun on TV.

Ben Strother

It was the first Monday in August, and I had just learned the Friday before that the Harris County grand jury had decided not to indict the policeman who shot my son. I had spent a miserable weekend worrying and cursing at that grand jury and God and everything else I could think of. I couldn't make up my mind whether to tell Doreen how it come out or not. I wasn't sure she'd understand either way, for one thing. She had gotten progressively more crazy over Joe Ben's death. She worried with that needlepoint in her hands all the time. She'd finished it a long time ago and then she'd tried to put it on the boy's picture and then she'd taken to carrying it around with her like a child will do a rag doll or a favorite blanket. It was stained and dirty, for she took it with her everywhere and often used it as a napkin and a handkerchief, too. She took to singing hymns all the time, too. Not loud or raucous, with great feeling, not like that. Just soft and nice so you could barely even hear her. She sang all the old ones we grew up with: "Let Us Gather at the River," "Rock of Ages," "Abide with Me." The one she kept going back to was "I Saw the Light." I don't know. And I worried, too, that if I did tell her and she did understand, that she might just go over the edge, if she hadn't already, or do something terrible. I mean, I had no idea what she might do.

She'd pretty much given up doing the housework and cooking. Not all of it at once or anything like that; just sort of gradually I began to notice things like dishes not being done or the bed not made, things like that. And cooking, she sort of tapered off on that, too. At first I'd eat from the icebox, whatever I could find, and then when that ran out I started getting stuff at the Dairy Queen and Colonel Sanders and places like that. Doreen would eat if I brought something home, but she never asked me for anything nor ever said she wanted anything if I asked her before I went out to get something.

Finally I took her to the doctor, and he said that such grief over the loss of a loved one was not that uncommon and he gave her some kind of medication to take, some kind of tranquilizer. That didn't make any sense at all to me, but then I'm not a doctor and I don't know. That medication never seemed to help, though; if anything, it seemed to me like she got worse; more depressed and more depressed. I never told her about the grand jury's decision that weekend. I did tell her later, however, and I guess, considering everything, she did understand what I was saying to her.

It was on that Monday, then, that I got this letter with the medical examiner's reports that I'd sent the fifteen dollars for back in June. And I got a letter, too, that Monday, from the Marine Corps, wanting to know if I knew the whereabouts of my son, that he had failed to report for induction. Before everything happened to Joe Ben, that's the kind of letter I would of answered even before I'd opened the rest of my mail; that's the kind of person I was. By that Monday, though, I wasn't the same as I'd been raised up to be. Something had happened not only to Joe Ben and to Doreen; something had happened to me, too. So all I did was crumple that Marine Corps letter up and throw it in the trash.

The medical examiner's reports, the autopsy and the toxicology reports, were something else altogether. Here I had just about given up. I had spent the weekend stewing about it and I had about come to the conclusion that it was all over; I had done everything I could do and it hadn't been enough. I'd even had an eyewitness to corroborate my suspicions about what had happened down in Rats Alley, and the grand jury had simply chosen to believe the policemen's version. I know why; I'm not blind. A little more than six months ago I would of voted the same way; I would of done the same thing. But I'd never had any experience before with that kind of thing. Now I had. And I knew there was a fix, a stonewall going on. You would think I would of learned my lesson with President Nixon, but I never.

The medical examiner's toxicology report confirmed what Burwitz had told me: Joe Ben had no drugs in him. There was no trace of alcohol and there was no trace of those Quaalude pills that the policemen claimed they found the packages of on the boy. The autopsy report confirmed also what I already knew, what Mr. McKee had told me at the funeral home the night last February when Doreen and I went out the first time to view the boy's body. The report said the shot that killed the boy had gone in the back of his head and then down into his brain. It also said there'd been a bullet wound on the boy's right hand, that had gone into the back of the hand and out the palm, as if the boy had been trying to protect himself in a hopeless way against the bullet from that policeman's gun. This was new information.

I studied on that and studied on that. It didn't square—couldn't square—with the testimony by the policeman. If Officer Kaprow had seen Joe Ben come out of the van holding a gun up over his head—which didn't make sense to me by itself, apart from everything else, to hold a gun up like that—and they had both rushed forward, and then he had shot the boy, how could the bullet go in from behind? And travel downward, too? Kaprow was big, but no bigger than Joe Ben. But the thing that was off, the thing that was wrong, was the bullet going in from behind. About the only way that could be true would be if Willie Valdeez or Birdy Shepherd's versions of what happened were true. And I knew again, as strong as I'd known it at any time during the previous six months, that I was right.

So instead of throwing in the towel, I called Leighton Burwitz long distance in the DA's office in Houston.

After we'd said our hellos, I asked him about the bullet going in the back of Joe Ben's head. He was silent. Then I asked him, "And how come is it that the medical examiner's autopsy report says Joe Ben had two wounds, one in his head and one in his hand, when the testimony of all four officers was that only one shot had been fired?" He did not answer me that one either. So I said, "I'll tell you a good explanation of how that happened, Mr. Burwitz. A good explanation is that the boy was trying to protect himself, in a panic, and that one bullet went through the boy's hand and then it went into his head and killed him. The policeman must have had his left hand restrained or something, and all he had free to bring up in a reflex protective action was his right hand, which clearly couldn't have had a gun in it or the bullet couldn't have gone through it like it did." I was silent for a moment and so was Burwitz. "Well," I said. "Doesn't any of this make you wonder? Make you the least bit curious that justice was not served?"

He was silent for a long time then. I thought he must of put the phone down or something. Then he said, "The medical examiner appeared before the grand jury and answered all questions and cleared up all problems, including those you've just posed."

"And?" I said.

"End of story," he said.

So that was that.

I could not restrain myself—did not *want* to restrain myself. I slammed the telephone down into the cradle.

I heard something in the distance, couldn't figure out what it was. I went to the door of our bedroom and listened down the hall. It was Doreen, singing one of her hymns; this time it was "There Is No Hope But Heaven Beyond This Vale of Tears."

I went back right away to the phone. I had to call Steve Rainey immediately. I could see now there was a lot of work I had to do if I was going to ever get justice done for my boy. I only thought I'd given up; hell, I was just getting started.

I don't know why I hadn't thought to do it before; what I asked Steve was, did Joe Ben have a gun or not the night he stole that van? That's the sort of question you'd normally expect the police to find out the answer to, but this wasn't normally.

"No," Steve said. "He never had no gun, Mr. Strother. He

never had no gun when he took that van and he never had one when they shot him, either, if you want my opinion."

Which was exactly what I thought.

So then I left the house and went downtown to see Sheriff Wilson.

"There *is* one other approach," he said.

"Yes?" I said.

"You could file a civil rights complaint on Joe Ben's death. That would bring the federal authorities into the picture. The FBI."

Well, I knew right away that was the thing to do. So I thanked Sheriff Wilson for the information and I went on back to the house. Then I got a shock. I couldn't find Doreen anywhere. My heart went up into my throat. She wasn't in the kitchen. I looked down the hall in the bedroom. She wasn't anywhere in the house. I was just about to call Sheriff Wilson when it hit me. So I tore out of the house and ran the few blocks to the church. And sure enough, that's where she was, sitting down at the front with her needlepoint in her hand, praying. I would of figured she'd wore out on that by now, but she still carried on with it.

I waited with her a few minutes and then I took her back home.

"It don't do no good," I told her.

"No more darkness," she said. "No more night."

After I got her settled down on the bed with a damp cloth on her forehead, then I went to the phone in the kitchen and called the United States attorney in Houston. I didn't speak with him, but I did speak with an assistant. He told me to write their office a letter telling them the facts in the case. I felt like I was getting the old runaround again, but there was nothing I could do. So I wrote them a letter. Then I copied it on the Xerox machine in the post office and I sent that copy to that newspaper fellow Shelby Satik that I'd met outside the grand jury room down in Houston back in the early part of the summer.

Sarah Jefferson

I had read and clipped the stories in the paper by Shelby Satik about the Strother boy. Then the same morning that I read an article about the boy's father writing the U.S. attorney's office and making a civil rights complaint, that same morning I got a call from Ben Díaz, the U.S. attorney and the man I work for; or rather, the man who appointed me head of the first Civil Rights Division in the U.S. attorney's office in Houston.

"I wrote Mr. Strother back and told him that a civil rights complaint had to be filed with the FBI rather than our office."

"Yes," I said. He knew I knew that was the appropriate procedure. He also knew that I knew he hadn't just called me to tell me that. "And?" I asked.

"And I want you to start someone in on this, OK? Something's off here; something's rotten."

"You can say that again," I said. I was overjoyed at the prospect of pursuing the matter. It had been bugging me for months. I mean the whole putrid mess of misuse of power at the level of the patrolman. I know they have rough jobs; I *know* that. What some of them don't seem to understand is they've got to be like Caesar's wife; they've got to be above even the suspicion of wrongdoing. It's a bitch, I agree; but that's the way it is, too.

"Sarah," Ben said.

"Yes?"

"I want to get to the truth here. If there has been any

wrongdoing, I want it found out. I want it revealed. I want indictments."

"Amen," I said.

"But if there's nothing there but smoke, I want that, too. This isn't a witch-hunt."

"Come on!" I said.

"OK, OK. Only I know you. And I know your office is a new one. And I know how anxious you are for a score."

"That's true, Ben," I said. "But it wouldn't do for the Civil Rights Division to go violating civil rights, now, would it?"

"That's right," he said. "You got anyone in mind to do this?"

"Yes," I said. "I do. At the risk of appearing to curry your favor."

"Who?"

"Hector Garcia."

"I don't know him."

"I just hired him."

"Good show."

"Civil Rights Division. He's first-rate, Ben. He'll stick like glue. He won't let go until after sundown."

"Well, unleash that Mexican, then."

We said our good-byes then and I buzzed Hector right away. In a moment he was in my office.

"What's up, Boss?" he said. He slid down into one of the easy chairs across from me and lit a cigarette. He was a little neater than usual that day, even had a tie on, I remember. Something got mixed up in his head when he was growing up in San Antonio. He became a lawyer, which isn't the most macho thing for a poor young Texas-Mexican to choose to be, and he paid absolutely no attention to his appearance. He was the anti-dude, if anything, only I don't think it was conscious. I used to accuse him of watching too many "Columbos" on television. Inside his head was where he was neat, though; that's where he was squared away.

So I explained the situation to him. I showed him the story Satik had in the paper that morning, and while he was reading it, I got my file of the newspaper stories Satik had been writing on the case all summer.

After Hector had read everything, he said, "Well, Shelby certainly seems to go along with the old man and the witness Valdeez."

"Yes," I said. "Amazing powers of observation you have there, Hector. To glean that information from purely objective news reports."

We both laughed.

"OK. I'll tell you what I think, Hector. I think that boy's gun was planted on him. And if you can find that out, I'll give you . . . something, I don't know what."

"How about a raise?"

"Cheeky bastard," I said. "You've only worked here a month."

"That's only as long as civil rights have existed in Harris County, Boss," he said.

"A medal," I said. "That's what I'll give you. With a medal and a quarter you can get a cup of coffee downstairs."

"No I can't," he said.

Hector took the file with him when he left and I sat down and wrote a letter to the local FBI office instructing those people to investigate the circumstances of the death of Joe Ben Strother. I gave that to my secretary to type and then I went downstairs for lunch.

The cottage cheese was old—not quite blinky but almost—and the lettuce was wilted. The ice tea was weak and there was no saccharin on the table. I support hiring the handicapped, and I appreciated that the blind guy who had the contract on the federal lunchroom might have been on welfare if he hadn't got preference in his concession bid because of his blindness. But he was also slow-witted, petulant, a lousy cook, and a cheat at the cash register. He'd pass a one for a five and a nickel for a quarter, going your way, and blame it on his blindness; but he never missed a number when it was money coming in. I had to fight the urge to try to cheat him every time I ate there. And every time I ate there I swore it was my last. It was good for my diet, though, because I never finished anything.

Just as I was leaving the lunchroom, Hector came in looking for me.

"Jesus Christ, Boss!" he said. His voice was pitched high with excitement.

"What?" I asked. "Calm down and tell."

"There's no question we got a live one," he said. "Everybody in on the thing is wired tighter than a Mickey Mouse watch."

"Good!" I said, genuinely warmed by our good fortune. "Good!"

Hector Garcia

We'd gotten enough information gathered by the time cold weather arrived to decide to take the case before a federal grand jury. So early in December we all gathered together in the name of the law and the federal guarantee of both the Fourteenth Amendment to the Constitution and the Civil Rights Act of 1964 to see if perhaps we could get down to the truth that we were pretty sure nobody had gotten to yet at the level of the state grand jury.

Kaprow and his running buddies got to give their version in detail of exactly what occurred that Saturday night in February months before.

"We were cruising on Loop 610 near the interchange to Interstate 45 East. We were heading toward town when we heard on the radio that a van had been stolen from a Dodge store out on the Loop. It wasn't minutes later that we seen, that we observed the suspect van heading in the opposite direction. It was being pursued at a high rate of speed by another police vehicle; that vehicle was manned by Officers Strunk and Ruiz." He nodded toward these two men.

"I exited at the first available offramp. It was my intention to go below, come under the freeway, and then regain access further up. I realized that I might lose the suspect and the other police cruiser, but I had no other option available to me if I was going to be of any use. When I got off the freeway, however, I found that the suspect and the cruiser chasing him had also exited the freeway and were still engaged in their chase down below. I came upon them, Officer Winkleman and me, at such a point as to allow us to come between the suspect and the other police vehicle."

"How did . . . ?"

"It was just an accident, how I come out down below. I just hit them in the middle, so to speak, as the van continued down side streets until it eventually come out on Cullen Road. Then it was the van first, then me and Winkleman, and then Strunk and Ruiz. We were going pretty fast a lot of the time by then."

"Until Cullen Road becomes Telephone Road."

"Yes. Lots of folks don't ever even call it that. Cullen Road."

"And then what occurred?"

"It was very wet. The pavement was slick still, even though it was not raining anymore by then. It was quite dangerous."

He was silent then. I decided not to say anything. It seemed to me that he was nervous, as if he were collecting himself for the part of the story that was an ordeal to him. It was the part of the story that had other versions to it than his own, so he had every reason to be apprehensive. He moved uncomfortably in the witness chair. I still did not speak. Finally, as if suddenly aware that he had been silent, he resumed his account.

"We turned off Telephone Road, following the van, onto a road down there they call Rats Alley. It . . . we saw several other vehicles, both coming and going, on Cullen Road and also further out on Telephone Road. Once down in Rats Alley we saw . . . I saw only one other vehicle and this was a Yellow Cab, number 1640, driven by a witness later identified as one Willie Valdeez. This vehicle was coming toward us but turned around and joined in the chase. I don't know how he managed to catch up to us; I suppose because we were forced to slow down considerably once we were down in Rats Alley. It is not an easy place to drive, particularly at high rates of speed and particularly at night when it has been raining."

"Please continue with the substantive portion of your account," I said. I figured if he was apprehensive that maybe I could needle him into carelessness and maybe shake his believability a little bit in front of the members of the jury. He did get angry, I could see it by his eyes, but he had done this testimony business too many times to give in with just that little touch of pressure. He wasn't going to be easy, but maybe he was breakable.

"Yes," he said. "I will. Pretty soon the suspect spun the van around, a full circle, 360 degrees, and the van stalled. It looked like he lost control of it at first, then like he decided to spin around only 180 and head back in the other direction. But then he appeared to have lost control . . ."

"This is of course all supposition?" I said, arching an eyebrow and showing my teeth.

"Yes!" Officer Kaprow said abruptly. "Of course it is. I don't know anything except what I saw the suspect do. I was in the car behind him. I have to assume these . . ."

"You know what they say about assumptions, don't you?" I asked him. His face colored slightly. And it ain't going to be me that gets made the ass of, either, I thought to myself. It's going to be you if it's going to be anybody. I sensed then I had got to him. He wasn't going to retain his cool in the face of clear badgering by an ethnic minority smart-ass. I had to do it, though; we were getting down to the nitty-gritty now.

"When the van stopped I managed to stop my cruiser, too. I jumped out of the car, drew my service revolver, and as I ran toward the van I fired a couple of warning shots. When I was within only a few feet from the van . . ."

"How many?" I asked, interrupting him.

"What?" he said. His eyes flamed.

"How many feet from the van were you?"

"I . . . I was about six feet from the van. Maybe less."

"OK. Go on. Then what happened?"

"When I was that close then, the suspect . . ."

"Joe Ben Strother."

"Yes, the suspect Joe Ben Strother." He mumbled across the name. "He exited from the van. I heard one of the guys behind me yell, 'Watch it! He's got a gun!' "

"Who was it?"

"I beg your pardon?"

"I say, who was it? Which of your fellow officers yelled 'Watch it! He's got a gun!' "

"I don't know," Kaprow said. "Under the stress of the circumstances I couldn't say for sure. I only know that one of them yelled it at me. And then I saw the gun myself. It was a large pistol. It turned out to be a Ruger revolver, that the suspect had. I was, of course, concerned for my safety and for the safety of my fellow officers. Therefore I attempted to subdue the suspect by talking to him. In the process of doing this, I shot the suspect."

"Where was the taxicab driver Willie Valdeez?" I asked. I pronounced "Valdeez" as Spanish as I could pronounce it, considering the spelling. He wasn't looking for the slider; his face registered confusion for just a moment. Then he got it.

"I'm not. . . . He was at the edge of the field on the far side of the road to my left. But I did not see him clearly. He was too far away. And I was pretty busy at the time."

So I tacked on him. A little change-up. Then a knuckleball. "In other words, when you heard someone behind you, a fellow officer, yell, 'He's got a gun!' and then you yourself saw the gun, still, even considering this fact, you went ahead and jumped him?"

He nodded, started to speak. I said, "A little foolhardy, wasn't it?" He colored again.

"Well," he said, shifting in his chair. "I was running toward the suspect . . ."

"Joe Ben Strother," I said.

"Joe Ben Strother," he said, almost firmly. "I was running toward him and it was too late for me to stop. I was too close. I couldn't really think of anything else. I was just functioning as I'd been trained. It was a reflex action. I didn't . . . it wasn't something I thought about, if you know what I mean."

"Yes," I said, sneering ever so slightly. "I think I do know what you mean." I waited another moment. "Let me see. I'm not sure I've got it exactly. Do you think you could go over once again the exact sequence of the tackling and shooting?"

"Yes," he said. It would have broken his mouth to say "sir" to me. "I'm not sure. I don't know, that is, exactly how we got into that position. I had him down on the ground. He was twisted around kind of, on his side." Kaprow contorted his own body just slightly. "As soon as we hit the ground there was someone right behind us, just behind us."

"And how long," I asked, striking, "how long was it then before you shot him?"

"I beg your pardon?"

"How long did you fight before you shot him?"

"Well. I had already shot him."

"When *did* you shoot him?"

"Well. Just as I grabbed him.

"Wait a minute!" I said loudly. "We'll have to go over this one more time." I had him now.

"That's exactly what I say," he said. "I don't know when I shot him. I shot him sometime between when I first seen him and. . . . Between then and when I closed with him. But it was *before* I tackled him. Yes. That's it. I would. . . . I shot him before I grabbed ahold of him. That's right. Before."

So that was that.

Joe Ben Strother was facing toward Kaprow. They were about the same height, only a scant few feet away from each other. Yet the bullet entered the top back of the boy's head and traveled downward into the brain and killed him. This part of the testimony was left in the hands of the medical examiner. I could wait. I was patient. I had done my part.

The day dragged on after that.

Obviously no one else was as impressed with my performance as I had been. As Kaprow and I both had been, I should say. The other three officers presented even more clearly defined pictures of the case. They, too, however, were "caught up in the heat of the moment" and thus unsure exactly when the shot had been fired. They couldn't see that well, they couldn't process the information they were receiving that fast, etc. They were, however, uniformly clear that the boy came out of the van carrying a gun in his right hand and that because of that, Officer Kaprow had done the right thing in shooting the suspect, something in fact they themselves were on the verge of doing had he not acted before they could act. Of the three,

Strunk seemed the most honest and the least comfortable. I figured, from my own private point of view, that it was because of his minority ethnic status in the presence of all those NWPs—not counting me and Officer Ruiz, who were, however, only NQWs. Officer Ruiz, though, tended to function more as a Native White Protestant than he did as Not Quite White. Of course, since I do the same myself, I certainly can't fault him for it.

After the hearing, I called Ben Strother back home. I told him the truth as I did every time I talked to him. It didn't really seem to matter to the grand jury when the boy was shot or where the bullet entered. They appeared to agree with the officers' contentions that the heat of battle may have obscured some details, fuzzed them, so to speak, but not the major ones. And the major ones boiled down really to two: suspect wrong, police right. The police were straight out of Jack Armstrong: clean, clean-cut, confidence-inspiring. The witnesses for what I was certain was the truth were not so authoritative. Valdeez was flat disreputable in his appearance. But he was telling the truth, and I knew it. I was less certain of Birdy Shepherd, but that was only because of the drinking.

"If I had your job with the U.S. attorney's office," Mr. Strother said, "I'd start putting the pressure on one of the policemen and see if one of them might just not crack."

I agreed, but my heart wasn't in it. I knew—thought I knew—that we needed more hard, irrefutable—*factual*—evidence for our case. A changed testimony is only as strong as the proof it reveals or is supported by.

I thought the gun was the weak place.

It came from somewhere.

If it was a throwdown, maybe its history would tell us what we needed to know.

About Doreen

. . . .

It was a Thursday, the week before Thanksgiving.

Ben was at work at the hardware store in the shopping center out off the traffic circle. Doreen had watched him wake up, shower and shave, dress, eat breakfast, and leave. It had all seemed to her like it was a dream. Everything had been like a dream, slipping into it gradually, from the moment she had first learned of Joe Ben's death by shooting in Houston, at the hands of Houston police. Seeing the boy's corpse in the coffin at the funeral home had freed her from fear, from the constraint of feeling as if her concern and worry were what held the world together, kept Joe Ben alive; but it had freed her also from practically every other connection to the shared life of reality.

She had given up her domestic duties, for the most part; from time to time she would get out the vacuum cleaner or unload or load the dishwasher, in a vain attempt to reconstruct the ordinary where—for her, with Joe Ben dead—it had ceased to exist. But then she would forget to use the vacuum, or she would line the dishes up on the kitchen counter and forget to put them away, or fail to turn on the dishwasher once she had it loaded. For the most part, she wandered the house as aimless in the movements of her body as she was aimless in the flow of the contents of her mind. She sang her hymns and kept moving, pausing periodically to wipe away some dust from a lamp table as she passed, using instead of her usual oiled cloth, the needlepoint she had long before constructed for what turned out to be no protection against the bullets of policemen.

At first Ben thought her condition would pass and so he was only mildly worried. After a while though, as the months went by it became clear that Doreen was slipping—had slipped—deeper and deeper into some faraway place uncomfortable and alien to his understanding. He became increasingly concerned about her. The doctor told him that a reaction such as hers was not uncommon. He prescribed a tranquilizer; it served only to make her slur her speech, when she had not before, and the words to the hymns she sang. It made her even further depressed, almost angry even. Ben took her to another doctor. He knew the story, of course, knew, too, the first doctor she had seen. He was his friend. He confirmed the first doctor's diagnosis, agreed with the prescription, upped the units, and sent her and Ben back home.

So the weeks and months had dragged along, into the heat of a central Texas summer, through the dog days, finally, of August, into the break that comes in October when the sky in Texas turns a dazzling color of blue, into the gray damp of November. And then a change—a subtle, tiny, but ever so real change—came over Doreen. At first Ben couldn't believe it; he thought his ears had deceived him. He listened more carefully; he had heard right the first time: periodically Doreen's hymns would turn inside out. Her paeans to Christ and to the Lord, her songs of praise to the Holy Ghost and to the three of them joined as one, became from time to time litanies of condemnation and blame, couched in the fiery language of hell. To hear her sing these black hymns both thrilled and terrified Ben Strother. Silently he shared her anger and resentment toward the Lord and toward the scheme of things that had so robbed him.

He thought he should take Doreen back to the doctors and tell them of the strange music he heard from her lips; but he could not bring himself to do so. He was too ashamed to admit to anyone what he had heard. And sometimes weeks would go by without her singing even one such Devil's hymn. Worst of all, he insisted on her regularly taking the tranquilizers and on assuring himself there was nothing to worry about; everything would be all right. Not even a wrathful God would take Doreen from him so soon after taking away his boy.

He didn't.

Doreen did it herself.

That Thursday in November, at approximately nine forty-five in the morning, as near as the county coroner could determine, Doreen Strother wandered back to the bedroom, dressed still in robe over pajamas and her fluffy worn mules, took Ben Strother's .45-caliber Colt automatic pistol from the night table on his side of the bed, and—with the knowledge of a country woman born into and raised in a world of guns—clicked off the safety catch, injected a round into the chamber, placed the barrel of the pistol in her mouth, and pulled the trigger with her thumb. In one thunderous moment Doreen left this life for whatever lies beyond it.

Ben found her when he came home at noon. There was surprisingly little blood around the room for the mess it made of Doreen. Released at last from her left hand was the soiled and worn "Jesus Saves" upon which she had kept afloat as long as she had. There was no identifiable, classifiable, expression on her face. The only visible mark left was the exit wound at the back of her head, like the small wound in her son's head, only quite large.

So everything stopped once more for Ben. School was out again. He numbed, stiffened, turned away. Then the pain came back, the great grief that strikes with death. He wept, and blamed himself for the doctors, the tranquilizers, and, most of all, for the gun.

Sheriff Wilson

Ben called me just as soon as he could get himself together and I went straight up to the house. I knew what he was feeling a little bit. I, too, have lost a wife and a son; but not together like that, in the space of less than a year.

She'd done a serious job of it, that's for certain; the bullet had entered the roof of her mouth, deflected, and come out the back of her head. Terrible wound, coming out. I collected the gun after I'd surveyed the situation and the coroner had looked things over. It was clearly self-inflicted. No one who knew Ben Strother would think for a moment he'd had anything to do with Doreen's death, that's for certain.

Ben looked better than Doreen, but not much. His face was flushed the way a face gets in August from the heat. After McKee had come and taken the body away, Ben started bleaching out. His face got white. It was the pain coming, the anger; the frustration that rises when the almost final rationale can no longer be uttered: *at least she's still alive.* After it, there is left only the final one: *at least I'm still alive.*

The deputy had taken all the pictures and run all the tests, measured and plotted, outlined and annotated. He took the gun in a plastic bag along with the spent round we had dug out of the wall just above the dresser.

Ben was still holding that needlepoint Doreen had done a long time ago and had had near her when she'd done what she had done. I gave her credit for the courage that I know it took, but I faulted her for doing it anyway. For courage isn't always the highest virtue, even so we're taught it is. Sometimes there is a greater courage hidden from us than the one revealed. It was too late for all that, however. She had done the thing. So final, so unretractable. So unfair.

We were in the living room together. I wasn't going to leave Ben for a while, even though I had checked and was pretty sure there were no other weapons around for him to act foolish with in his grief. He said he didn't need me to stay, which I knew was right. He didn't need me to, but I thought it was a good idea anyway.

"I just can't understand," he said. "What have I done for the Lord to punish me this way?"

"I understand your feelings, Ben," I said. "But it wasn't you. I mean, these things just happen to human beings because they're human beings. There wasn't anything you could have done."

"I know," he said. He was silent for a while. Then suddenly he cried, "Oh God! She's gone! Her and the boy both are gone!" His shoulders shook with grief and he covered his face with his hands. There's nothing you can say, I know, to ease the pain. It's just the talking. The sound of another human's voice, another one who is still alive, still in the race, still carrying the burden; that's all it is. Just the whisper of living up against the roar of death.

And so I talked and talked and little by little Ben calmed down as he began to let it be the truth that now Doreen, too, was gone and there was only him against the world. I swear that for a moment I wanted to hold him like a child and let him cry himself dry, until he fell asleep against my shoulder. I couldn't do that, of course, and he wouldn't have wanted it.

Saturday morning we buried her in a plot next to the boy. There wasn't quite so many people at her services as there had been at the boy's, but then he had been in school and knew so many more folks. He had been young and his death had shocked us all. She had been still alive then, and I imagine many people came to the boy's funeral because of sympathy for her, a mother who had lost her son. I can't imagine that it's any easier for a father, judging from my own experience, but then I'll never know the answer to that. There were no services in the church for Doreen, either. Ben just had services at the grave. It was cold under the canvas awning McKee had set up, and it rained, and the sound of the rain on the awning mixed with the gray cold of the day to tell us all was not well, that life sometimes was, Lord knows, a burden. Over us all hung the knowledge that poor Doreen, unlike those of us present at her funeral, had come to the conclusion—mad though she may have been in reaching it—that the burden wasn't worth carrying. And she had laid it down on her own; hadn't waited for God to lift it. I could understand. I wondered if Ben could.

I wanted him to come to my place after the funeral, but he said he'd better go on home. There wasn't anything planned there that I knew of, so I gathered together a few people, the Higleys and Janelle from the church, and Martha, my wife, and some of the others, and we all invited ourselves home with him. I wasn't going to have him alone on that day. After we'd all got there and put some coffee on and the ladies were cleaning up, straightening up and poking into things, I slipped out and went to the store and got some food and then went by the office and got a bottle of Jack Daniels, and then went on back. It took till about dark to get Ben to take a drink, but when he finally did he couldn't get enough and I had him in bed asleep—drunk, but asleep—by eleven o'clock that night. There wasn't nobody left around then but me and my wife. She took the car home and I stretched out on the couch. I didn't want him alone even then.

Of course, I couldn't stay with him forever; I knew that. And he seemed all right to me enough by the next day that I went on home. The Higleys were back over by then, in the afternoon after church, with fried chicken and all the trimmings.

By the end of the next week he seemed almost back to normal to me.

I should have known better.

Hector Garcia

On one of the first few working days of the new year, Sarah Jefferson called me to her office and instructed me to close out the Strother case. There were more pressing matters for our division, she said, and the case seemed stalled. She agreed with me that there *was* a throwdown in the case, but she also pointed out that we were stuck.

"Look," I said, "give me some time. I'm working on it. I'm working on the gun."

"Díaz already gave me the word to shut it down," she said.

"Call him," I said. "Right now. Call him right now and ask him for more time." I looked as soulful as I could. I hate to use my charms like that, but I was desperate.

"Oh, all right," she said, shrugging her shoulders. "What could it hurt?"

She dialed and they exchanged pleasantries a moment. Then she said, "Look, Ben. Hector is here in the office. He wants just a little more time on the Strother case." She was silent a moment. Then she handed me the phone. "He wants to talk to you," she said. I was nervous. I didn't have that much to do with Mr. Big on my own, and I wasn't comfortable having to talk to him. I didn't have much choice, though, so I took the phone.

"Hello," I said. "Look. I know what you said. Sarah just told me. But I would like to follow one more lead, OK?"

"What's that?" he asked. His tone was not unfriendly.

"The gun. The throwdown. I want to trace that gun all the way back to the factory. I want to confirm the police report."

Díaz didn't speak for a moment; I could almost hear the wheels turning.

Finally he said, "OK. But make it fast, OK? We got a lot of stuff piling up."

"You bet," I said. Then I added, "Thanks, Ben."

"Sure," he said. His voice was positively friendly. The U.S. attorney had a heart!

When I hung up I was smiling from one side of my handsome face to the other.

"I assume that grin of yours means he said yes," said Sarah. I leaned down and kissed her on the forehead.

"You got it, kid," I said.

"Don't let the doorknob hit you in the ass," Sarah said. God, I liked her.

So I was on my way.

I went back to the office, called the Houston Police Department and got permission to come by and pick up the paperwork they had on the gun. I was there before the tone signal resumed.

The thing that interested me mainly was the report on the gun prepared by the U.S. Bureau of Alcohol, Tobacco, and Firearms. According to that report, the gun—a Single Six model, .22-caliber single-action revolver—had been manufactured by the Sturm, Ruger and Company, Inc., firearms plant in Southport, Connecticut, and had been shipped to a wholesaler in Houston, which had in turn sold the gun to a store in south Houston. In 1965 that store—a Globe's Discount Store—had shipped the gun to another Globe store, a new one in north Houston.

There was a problem there. A purely coincidental piece of information revealed it to me immediately. My girl—my ex-girl, that is—used to live in north Houston. Her house was just a few blocks from that Globe Discount Store. I remember that when I first started dating her in 1975 they were just building that store. In fact, I remember that they had a big grand opening that spring, because I remember the searchlights at night that used to make my girl's dog bark like crazy every time they scraped across the sky. We bought beer there a couple of times to take with us when we went fishing. So, what I knew was that the report on the gun by the Bureau of Alcohol, Tobacco, and Firearms was wrong. Because it had the gun being shipped to that particular store in north Houston almost a decade before there was such a store. The report was wrong. I was elated. I knew something big that January morning and it was pure luck that I did. But I wasn't going to tell Sarah anything about it until I could demonstrate what my brains, skill, and determination could do with that good fortune.

I saw no point in going to the Globe store in north Houston to check their gun sales records. I was prudent enough, though, to check with them to find out when they'd originally opened. I was right, they had opened in April of 1975. The next step back on the ladder then was the other Globe, the one in south Houston.

I got there just after lunch. I went straight to the back to the administrative offices, showed my credentials, waited while the manager made a phone call to Sarah, then was led into a back conference room. After a few moments by myself, I was rejoined by the manager, carrying a big dusty box.

"Here they are, Mr. Garcia," he said. "I'm afraid we don't have this stuff on microcards yet."

"No problem," I said. "This may all be a wild goose chase anyway."

"Well, good luck," he said. "If you need anything, paper or pencil or coffee or anything, just give one of the girls a yell, OK?"

"You bet," I said. He was clearly unaware of the civil rights violation he'd just committed in principle.

So I took off my jacket and set to work. I had the serial number of the pistol reputedly found in the boy's hand. I put that piece of paper out on the big long conference table to my right. Then I took the top off the black and white speckled cardboard box and put it back away to my upper left. I took a good handful of those four-by-six-inch cards from the front of the box, and started in looking at numbers. I had the gun sale records from that particular store for the year 1965. The first sale was January 4. That's because the fourth was a Monday and thus the first day the place was open for business after the long weekend. Anyway, whatever the reason, Monday the fourth was the date of the first sale, but the number of the gun wasn't the same as the number I was looking for. The day had just begun.

It was the hardest part of the whole case for me. First, there was the problem of simply paying attention. I would realize from time to time that I had picked up and pretended to scan as many as ten or twelve of those cards without seeing a thing on them. It reminded me of reading poetry assignments in high school.

So I'd have to go back through the cards until I found the last one I'd really looked at, and then start forward again. Paying attention is not an easy thing to do, even for someone who does it for a living, like me. You have to work at it all the time in order to be intentional, I guess you could say.

That went on for hours.

Then finally, after more than a thousand cards—think how many guns must have been sold in the whole United States in 1965—finally, I was a sweepstakes winner. I wasn't certain to be; the flaw in the bureau report could have occurred at the level of the wholesaler, not at the level of Globe's at all. So God was with me again.

According to the record-of-sale card, the pistol alleged to have been found in Joe Ben Strother's hand after he had been shot by Officer Eldon Kaprow, almost a year before, had been bought in September of 1965 by a man who had given his name as Raymond Germany. Unless he was a pretty sophisticated criminal with an illegal driver's license and other illegal identification cards, the chances were good that was his real name.

I went out of the conference room and found one of the "girls."

"Can I borrow your phone book?" I asked.

"Oh, yes, sir," she said. She studied me closely. I know I'm sloppy, but I still think it's bad manners for them to stare at me the way they do sometimes. Of course, she might have been staring at me because I'm so good-looking.

She handed me the phone book from a side drawer in her desk. I handed her the register-of-sale card on the gun. "Could you Xerox me a copy of this?" I asked.

"Oh, yes, sir," she said. God knows who that manager told her I was.

While she did that, I opened the Houston phone book and looked up Raymond Germany. I didn't find exactly what I wanted, but I found a Raymond Germany, Jr. The secretary wasn't back yet, so I went ahead and dialed the number.

A little girl answered. "Is your daddy there?" I asked.

"No," she said sweetly. "But my mama is."

I waited a little.

"Can I speak to her?" I asked when I realized she was still waiting.

"Yes," she said. Then she either threw the phone down on a hard plastic tabletop or hit it with a rock: the bang almost broke my eardrum. Directly a grown-up answered.

"Hello," she said.

"Hello," I said. "My name is Hector Garcia. I am a staff lawyer with the Civil Rights Division of the U.S. attorney's office here in Houston."

"Yes," she said. Her voice was guarded, suspicious. Nothing new. "What can I do for you?"

"I'm trying to locate Mr. Raymond Germany," I said. "But I don't think it's Raymond, Jr. The man I'm trying to locate is a man who bought a gun from a Globe Discount Store back in 1965."

There was a long silence.

Finally, the woman spoke again. "That wouldn't be Ray, Jr.," she said. "You're right about that. That would be Ray, Sr."

I wondered how she could be so sure.

"Because," she said. "Ray, Sr., bought that gun and shot himself with it, killed himself, in 1965."

"Committed suicide?"

"That's right. He committed suicide."

She was silent again.

"OK," I said. "Listen. I'm very sorry to bring this up again.

know it must be painful for you. If you'd like, I can make an appointment and come to your house so you can see my credentials."

"No," she said, flatly. "It's all right. It's been a long time ago, now. I'd rather just tell you what you want to know. It doesn't matter who you are, even if you aren't . . . you know, Civil Rights whatever it is."

"What happened to the gun then? Do you know?"

"Yes," she said. "No. Ray . . . Ray, Jr., said he didn't want it. So after they were through with it, they just kept it. I guess they done something with it."

"Yes, ma'am," I said. "Well. I guess that's it."

She said nothing.

"I appreciate this very much," I said. "Thank you."

"It's OK," she said. "I think about it all the time anyway. So does Ray. We don't know why he done it. There wasn't a note or nothing. We never have known why, and we've just always wondered."

"I'm quite sure," I said, thinking back to the recent suicide of Mrs. Strother. I wasn't quite sure why she did it, either. She, too, left no note. Yet I knew perfectly well why, at the same time. "I guess there are just some things we have to leave to God," I said.

"That's right," she said. "That's surely right."

We said good-bye then and hung up.

All of a sudden my victories of the day didn't seem so important anymore. All of a sudden everything was very personal, very tactical, very dark. There was no big picture, all of a sudden. All of a sudden there were just poor sad desperate lives, survivors defending their pitiful scanty turf, with no hope of winning, ever.

By the time the girl got back with the Xerox copies, I was ready to go drinking.

But I didn't.

Instead, I instructed her to keep that sales record available because I was going to subpoena it, and I put on my jacket and sunglasses and left. My next stop was back at the Houston Police Department.

That's where my speedy successes ended.

I spent the next three and a half days in a records warehouse, searching through moldy boxes of papers without any real hope of finding anything. What a pain in the ass that was. But nothing is free in this life, and the world is, after all, round. I mean, I was *given* the Globe Discount Store in north Houston, and it took me only a few hours at the store in south Houston to find the record-of-sale. So it was only right that it take me days to locate the suicide report on Raymond Germany, Sr.

Finally I did, though.

Finding 1965 was a rough job by itself; finding that particular report in the 1965 stash was even worse. I'm a born slave, though; otherwise I'd have never made it through law school. I just kept plugging away, plugging away, grabbing myself by the ear and forcing myself to pay attention and sure enough, because doggéd *does* do it, I found it. There it was, bigger than Texas and twice as pretty.

The pistol identified as the one used by Raymond Germany, Sr., to shoot himself in the right temple was the same make and model as the one found next to Joe Ben Strother down in Rats Alley. What's more—and more important—the serial numbers of those two pistols were exactly the same. Disposition of the gun? It had been confiscated by the Houston Police Department.

Things were starting to look awfully gloomy for Officers Kaprow, Winkleman, Strunk, and Ruiz. Things were starting to look a whole lot better for justice.

The Break

Part One

Hector Garcia wasted no time in reporting his discoveries to his superior Sarah Jefferson. She was as elated as he was by his findings. It was clear that the new Civil Rights Division of the U.S. attorney's office—*her* division—was on its way. It would be a power in Houston law enforcement circles.

"Come on," she said. "We won't call Ben. We'll go tell him face-to-face."

Together she and Hector went down the long hall to the office of U.S. Attorney Benito Juárez Díaz.

After he had heard their story, Díaz immediately picked up his phone and called Shirley Boudreaux, chief of the Houston Police Department. He explained everything to Boudreaux and then suggested, "Perhaps Internal Affairs would like to look into this matter, don't you think, Shirley?"

Shirley agreed.

He clicked the plunger down as soon as he was through talking to Díaz and dialed the office of Detective Santiago Cruz, head of Internal Affairs for the Houston Police Department.

By the middle of the following week, Internal Affairs had completed its investigation and made its report. The report said that the gun in question had been melted down in 1969, along with other such confiscated weapons. As far as Internal Affairs could figure out, someone had simply lied, because it was obvious enough that the gun had not been melted down. The

Internal Affairs team had in fact seen the gun, held now in the Houston Police Department as evidence yet to be disposed of until the complete resolution of the Strother shooting incident, which meant until the Civil Rights Division finished its investigation.

Shelby Satik had a story on the gun in the paper on the Sunday following the Internal Affairs discovery. Now everyone in Houston and half of the rest of Texas knew all there was to know about the case except one thing: what exactly did happen down in Rats Alley more than a year before?

Back together in her office, Sarah Jefferson and Hector Garcia sat at her desk with coffee cups filled two fingers deep with sour mash whiskey.

"We ain't won it, yet," Sarah said. "But we're mighty close."

They both laughed.

"What now?" she asked Hector.

"You got no plan?" he asked her.

"I think I do," she said. "But you're much closer than I am on this. I would much rather hear your idea first."

"Well, it's not too sophisticated. But I think it's a place to start."

"Yeah?"

"There was this one guy. One of the four policemen. William Strunk. You remember him?"

Sarah nodded.

"There was something about him. I'm not sure. I think Ben Strother saw it, too. He doesn't seem at all comfortable about what's going down. I mean, we get a steel wall from Kaprow and the other two, Winkleman and Ruiz. But Strunk; he's different. He doesn't really seem to be a part of all of this."

Sarah started to speak but Hector interrupted her. "Yeah. I know, I know. He *is* a part of it. He's gone along with the rest all right. But have you paid attention to him during the hearings? He is with them in a way, but he's not, either, in another. It seems to me. . . ." Hector got up, took his cup of whiskey with him, started pacing around the room. "Look. I remember when I first knew I was going on to high school. There were a lot of guys, friends of mine that I still hung around with for a while after that. They weren't going to go to high school, see. And pretty soon, after I was in high school, we did stop hanging around together. The same with college, and especially—*doubly*—the same with law school. My point is, we had a shared past, a shared life, that we both continued with even after the die was cast to change that shared life forever. It's like, Strunk is in this because he can't help himself. He's riding on their shared past together, his and Kaprow's or his and his partner Ruiz's. Who knows? But I get the definite feeling that he wishes he was a million miles away from all this."

He was quiet a moment. "And pretty soon that shared past, that shared life as policemen, is going to recede into a past that he can't see, or remember, or recall the significance of. I mean, he's going to go on to be a black civilian, and they're not; and here, now, that means separate ways. If we win, that is."

"OK," said Sarah Jefferson. She was sitting back in her big executive's chair with her feet up on the desk, sipping her whiskey. "Let's call him in."

Hector smiled and then sat down again. "What was your idea?" he asked, taking a sip himself from his cup.

"Shoot the sons of bitches!" she said soberly. Then she laughed. "Just kidding, of course," she said. "But, oh God, if they are guilty, somebody ought to."

"That's not civil rights talk," said Hector, laughing. "But I hear what you're saying; I hear where you're coming from."

So early on Monday morning they called Officer William Strunk into Sarah Jefferson's office, thinking that the Civil Rights Division nameplate on her door might be useful to their interrogation.

At precisely ten o'clock, Officer Strunk knocked on Sarah Jefferson's door.

"Come in," she called.

Hector Garcia was standing by Sarah's desk. She was seated behind it, dressed in a dark gray tailored suit. Her blue-gray hair was pulled back in a severe bun. Her round steel-rimmed glasses and her lined and taut face made her look formidable. Hector Garcia had worked at it himself. He had a coat and tie on, his shirt was tucked in, his hair was combed, and his shoes were polished. Neither he nor Sarah smiled.

Officer Strunk looked like an advertisement for the police academy. His uniform was pressed and clean and fit him like it was tailored. His footgear and other leather shone softly in the gray morning light that filtered through the yellow Houston haze. He had his headgear under his arm and stood at attention just inside the door.

Hector walked toward him as if to greet him, but instead went behind him and closed the door firmly, and then switched on the overhead lights. Suddenly all of the softness drained from the room.

"Have a seat," Sarah said in a technically neutral tone, tinged nonetheless with steel-gray ice.

Officer Strunk came forward and sat in the chair she indicated, directly in front of her desk, about five feet away.

"Go ahead," she said to Hector Garcia, who in turn began to recite: "You have the right to remain silent. Anything you say can be used against you in a court of law. You have the right to have an attorney present during any questioning. If you cannot afford to hire an attorney, one will be furnished for you free of charge. If you waive these rights, you may revoke that waiver at any point of questioning. Do you understand these rights?"

He nodded.

"Look," said Sarah Jefferson, her steel rims flashing now under the bright fluorescent lights. "We want to know . . . we *need* to know exactly what happened, what *really* happened down in Rats Alley last February."

"You've. . . . I think the statements of both myself and the other officers. And, of course, the judgments of No Bill rendered by both grand juries. It seems to me, under the circumstances . . ."

"No," said Hector. "It won't wash anymore, Strunk. Look. You, of all of those men, how can you let such a flagrant violation of that boy's civil rights occur? What about you if the police in this town can dispose of Joe Campos Torres and Joe Ben Strother with impunity? You think the blacks in Fifth Ward aren't going to suffer the fallout from garbage like this?"

"I've. . . . No one has to tell me my job. I've been a policeman for almost twenty years. And I can only say, as I've said, the reports have been in. They've been looked at by the . . . you know. Internal Affairs as well as the grand juries. It might. This could be . . . harassment. You . . ."

Then there was silence for a long time. In spite of the chilliness in the room, Officer Strunk was sweating heavily. He was not comfortable in the chair, no matter how much he shifted about to make himself so. His eyes could not find the right place to light.

After some long moments, Garcia asked, "Do you want to call a lawyer?"

"No," said Strunk.

"Do you want to call anyone?" asked Sarah.

"No, no," said Strunk, shifting about. "It's just. Look. There are so many people involved here, not just me. So many lives."

"Did you know, by the way," asked Garcia, settling back against the front of Sarah's desk, on the left side, "that the boy's mother killed herself."

Strunk's head drooped. "Yes," he said. "I heard that."

Again there was a lengthy silence.

Only the sounds of auto traffic far below kept the three in touch outside themselves.

"Well," said Strunk finally. "I guess it's over, then."

"Go on," said Sarah Jefferson softly.

"The boy had no gun. He wasn't armed. Ruiz and I pulled up just after Kaprow and Winkleman got there. They both came out of the car fast, heading straight for the driver's side. When the boy came out, they both were on him, all over him. They threw him down, knocked him down. Then Winkleman ran around the van, I guess to see if anyone else was there. Then Kaprow. . . . I don't know how it happened. He was on the boy. And Valdeez, the taxicab driver, was coming from across the road near a field on the far side. Kaprow had his service revolver out. I heard a shot go off. Then Winkleman came back around the van. Ruiz and I yelled at the taxicab driver, Valdeez, to get out of there. Winkleman was hollering at him to come back. He kept going. We all come up and stood around then. The boy's body was twitching. Like, you know, a chicken. They'll be dead, but their body still moves. Jerks and twitches." He fell silent.

"And then?" asked Garcia.

All of a sudden it looked just as if Strunk awoke from a trance.

"What?" he asked.

"And then what happened?" asked Sarah Jefferson.

"I. . . . I have nothing else to say. I want to call a lawyer."

"Wait a minute," said Garcia. "You . . ."

"No," said Sarah Jefferson. "That's right. You go ahead. But I want you back in this office at three o'clock this afternoon, with your lawyer present. Do you understand?"

"Yes, ma'am," said Strunk.

Part Two

That afternoon at precisely 3:00 Strunk returned with his lawyer, O'Brian Lefkowitz, and his wife, Suzie, and their preacher.

"What I'd like to do here if I could," said Lefkowitz to Sarah Jefferson and Hector Garcia, "is to make some kind of agreement with you folks."

"Yes," said Sarah. "We're prepared to listen." Hector started to speak but Sarah caught his eye and frowned and he bit his lip.

"Our position is this," said Lefkowitz. "If Officer Strunk here tells the truth about what happened that night, if he does that in front of the federal grand jury, then your office will grant him immunity from prosecution."

"You realize," said Sarah, "that I can't make that bargain with you. That's a bargain that only the U.S. attorney, Ben Díaz, can make."

"I realize," said Lefkowitz. "I realize also that Sarah Jefferson runs the Civil Rights Division and that if she asks Ben Díaz to make this agreement, he will do so."

"I can't say with certainty that he will," Sarah said.

"Look. All I want is your word that you will seek the agreement."

Sarah waited a moment before speaking. She studied Lefkowitz carefully. Finally she said, "OK. You got a deal." She and Lefkowitz shook hands. Hector Garcia was up from his chair now, in a far corner of the room, pouting.

Part Three

"And then?" asked Garcia. Everyone on the grand jury panel was paying attention.

Officer Strunk continued, "Kaprow jumped back then, stood up and jumped back away from the boy. I was right there by them. I knelt down quickly to see if the boy . . . "

"Joe Ben Strother."

"Yes. To see if Joe Ben Strother had been hit by the round Kaprow had fired or not. Maybe not, I thought. Then I looked up to my left and I saw the cab driver approaching. I yelled at him to get away, to get back. He stopped in his tracks for a minute, and then he turned around and ran back to his cab. Winkleman had gone to the van and he was coming back around now and I heard him yelling at the cab driver to stop, to come back. But he didn't, he just kept going."

"And what about Joe Ben Strother?"

"Well, the bullet had hit him, all right. I saw the boy was going to die. I mean, he didn't last more than five to ten minutes. So we asked Kaprow, 'What do you want to do? Do you want to use a gun, or do you want . . . you know, just to stop it right here?' I don't. . . . It's easy to condemn him for what he done. And it's easy to condemn us, too. But you have to visualize the situation. You have to remember the conditions. There was an awful lot of adrenaline flowing. I'm not condoning . . . "

"Please," said Hector Garcia. "Please. Just tell the jury what transpired. The physical part of what transpired, OK?"

"Yes, sir," said Strunk. "So Kaprow said, 'Yes,' and nodded his head. He was in shock over it already." Strunk was silent then. He stared off at the floor in front of him.

"Who put the gun down next to the body?" Garcia asked.

"Winkleman did," said Strunk. His voice was barely audible.

"Who did?" asked Garcia. "I'm afraid I didn't hear you."

"Officer Jerome Winkleman did," said Strunk, this time more loudly. "Officer Winkleman."

"And where did he get the gun?" asked Garcia.

"It was in the patrol car. His and Kaprow's."

"Why did they have a throwdown in their car? Were they planning something like this?"

"No. I mean, I don't know. Winkleman had been doing some target shooting, or was going to with his kids. He just forgot he had the gun. And he said he was afraid to leave it in his private vehicle while he was on duty. He was afraid someone might steal it."

At this, some members of the grand jury laughed. Those who did not laugh looked disapprovingly at those who did.

"But what about the cab driver? Didn't any of you wonder whether you could get away with planting a throwdown on the boy after there'd been a witness that saw he had no weapon when he was shot?"

"Yes, we did discuss that. We concluded that, under the circumstances of the night and the quickness and the violence, the rain. He couldn't be certain what he saw. And. . . . "

"And what?"

"And we figured our word would be taken before his would. Since there were four of us."

"And since you were policemen."

"And that, too, yes."

"And since he was racially marginal."

"That didn't enter my mind. I couldn't see. I don't know about the others."

"I imagine not," Garcia said. There may have been a plea bargain, but he was going to get his pound of flesh, anyway. "So. Go on."

"So Officer Winkleman went to the patrol car and got the throwdown. One of us, I'm not sure who, had some Quaalude wrappers, too, so we put them in the boy's pocket."

"In Joe Ben Strother's pocket."

"That's correct."

"And?"

"And we thought, What if they run a trace-metal test on his hand to see if he held the gun? So we couldn't just put it down there. We had to wrap his hand around it."

"While he was still alive."

"That's right. He was groaning and still moving some."

"And then what did you do?"

"And then Officer Ruiz went to our cruiser and called for an ambulance to come."

Part Four

The next day Jimmy Lambert, the law-and-order witness who had testified that he had seen what the officers had originally said had happened, admitted under intense questioning by the FBI that he had in fact arrived on the scene, on his way to work, after the shooting, and that what he *had* seen was the boy lying on the pavement with a gun in his hand. He had not, in fact, seen what led up to that. He was indicted for perjury.

That same next day, Officers Strunk, Kaprow, Winkleman, and Ruiz were fired from the Houston Police Department by Chief Shirley Boudreaux.

By the time the buds came on the trees and the birds started chirping again, the federal grand jury had indicted Kaprow, Winkleman, and Ruiz.

Kaprow was charged with a civil rights violation, while acting "under color of the laws of the State of Texas" to deprive Joe Ben Strother of his life and liberty in violation of the Fourteenth Amendment to the U.S. Constitution, the Equal Protection Amendment.

Winkleman was charged with the offense of securing and physically placing the throwdown gun on Joe Ben Strother's body with the intent to deceive.

Ruiz was charged with aiding and abetting and failing to tell the truth about what had happened that night.

And, in addition, all three were accused of conspiracy. They had agreed to hide the facts and to lie before two grand juries.

The trial was set for later that summer.

Ben Strother

The boy is dead.
His mother is dead.
What satisfaction can I possibly have that will make up even partly for the pain I feel at those losses? None. No one, either. Just me, by myself, here in this house, that used to be my home.
  Mr. Garcia called this morning to tell me the federal grand jury had indicted three of those policemen. I asked why not the fourth? And what about those detectives, Gates and Sanborn? I asked about Burwitz, too, the assistant district attorney. Why not him? He believed the policemen. He was willing to let them sweep it all under the carpet, to cancel out the fact of the murder of my son. Of course, if he had been successful. Or if I had not persisted, then maybe Mother would be alive today. Maybe if I had just let sleeping dogs. . . . But I could not. I would have done so if I could. But I could not.
  It's funny, the one who came forward, that Willie Valdeez. I wouldn't have allowed him on my property before. And I would have trusted my life to those policemen, to Burwitz, to all of them. Isn't that funny. What we think is the truth turns out to be a lie, and what we think a lie, the truth. Except for people like Mrs. Jefferson, and Hector Garcia. I used to think they were all like them, and Mr. Díaz, the U.S. attorney. It's not right that there should be only a few of their kind and so many of the others. Although I guess I can understand it, in a way. They acted just like the boy did. Impetuous, without

thinking. Then afraid and alone. Only he was just a boy, not really old enough to have good sense, much less to use it if he did. And so they killed him, for nothing. And then his mother. And what for? For her, nothing, too. Just black nothing.

So after I talked to Garcia I went down the hall toward the bedroom. Our bedroom, it used to be. I paused, though, at the door to his bedroom. That used to be. I saw the puzzle there on his desk, all the yellow wooden pencils, that I'd started working on so long before, the very weekend it all happened to the boy. I had not even been in his room since Mother died. I crossed to the desk and looked down at the puzzle. It was covered with dust. I wiped across it absently with my fingers, then brought them up and studied the little semicircle waves of dust that gathered on my fingertips, collected past the edge of pressure on the puzzle board. I searched then for a piece, part of one of the erasers, but my attention wavered, my mind went away from the problem. I picked up a piece or two of the puzzle at random and tried them in open slots that my eye told me clearly they could not fit. It was mechanical. I never liked puzzles anyway. But I usually finished what I started. Right then I couldn't have argued that to do so was a virtue; I can't say I felt I had gained much from my most recent, and my greatest test of patience, of endurance. What had it all proved? Nothing, that's what.

Well, at least there would be a trial. At least three of the policemen, including the one who pulled the trigger, would get some kind of punishment for what they'd done. It had already started, in fact; the punishment: they were no longer Houston policemen. Unfortunately, that all came too late to spare my family. But at least it came; at least they couldn't do again what they had done to Joe Ben. And they—or I—to his mother. It's all so strange. Who could ever figure out where it all started? The tiny act that caused another that caused another that led to stealing the van, to his death, to Doreen's, and to . . . who knows what else to come?

Because I know one thing if I don't know any other. If those three policemen are found innocent or just rapped across the knuckles, then. . . . Then I don't know. But I do know I demand some punishment, something . . . something meaningful. There has to be something in all this somewhere that means something. It can't all be just for nothing.

So. I figured I might as well put the pieces of that puzzle away, for I knew I wasn't ever going to finish that thing. Partly I must have just been showing off for Mother. No more of that. So I got the box bottom and slid all the puzzle pieces into it and made sure those that I'd managed to connect were all separated. Then I covered the box and put it up into Joe Ben's closet, on a shelf at the back.

I looked around the room.

It was still the same.

I wondered if I ought to change it; throw out the furniture, give all the boy's things away, take down the pictures. Get rid of all the reminders that made my heart ache as I looked around at them. And I wondered the same about Mother's things. I'd done nothing, and it had been a long time, even for her. I wish she'd just left a little note, saying something. Some explanation, some word.

Maybe, maybe not. There wasn't any point in getting in a big hurry. Things have a way of taking care of themselves, working themselves out.

Then I went on out of the boy's room and finished getting dressed and went on to work at the hardware store. Sometimes the best thing to do is simply to watch and wait.

The Trial

The case came to trial in late July, almost a year and a half after Joe Ben Strother stole the van and was killed. It lasted nine weeks. U.S. District Court Judge Hazard Addison presided.

Kaprow's lawyers, Max Lebensold and Earl Pratt, came out swinging. They contended that perhaps Strunk or Ruiz or Winkleman had shot Joe Ben Strother. They charged, obliquely but surely, that the government's witnesses were tainted because one of them had gotten his immunity from prosecution through his testimony. That was Strunk, of course. They were outraged by such a thing! They attempted also to tar Winkleman and Ruiz with the same brush. Birdy Shepherd's testimony was unacceptable, they said, because he had been drinking. Willie Valdeez was an untrustworthy witness, they implied, because his hair looked like a used Brillo pad. They never so much as mentioned the tainted—and indicted—Jim Lambert. They contended that the government's version of the shooting was a fairy tale with organic inconsistencies. There was too much in the government's version that didn't fit into a neat little paradigm as did the testimony of the four policemen. Furthermore, and finally, everything had happened so quickly it was highly unlikely that the officers had had the time to hatch a conspiracy and carry it out before others arrived on the scene. Ruiz was an excellent defense witness. Winkleman did not take the stand.

The prosecution had what it considered to be the truth on its side. It wasn't nearly as offensive as the defense, in the sense that it did not attack so aggressively. It bided its time; it had the truth. It also had the testimony of Officer William Strunk.

Judge Addison explained his charge to the jury during a Friday afternoon session in early September. Already the fog lingered with an autumnal aura under the pine trees in the Harris County mornings. The jury filed out, was sequestered. It did not appear again until the following Friday. Ben Strother sat in the back of the courtroom next to Shelby Satik from the newspaper and Willie Valdeez. Birdy Shepherd did not return to court after his testimony. Neither did Officer Strunk. The judge called upon the foreman to read the jury's verdict.

It found Eldon Kaprow innocent of the charge of violating the civil rights of Joe Ben Strother.

It found Eldon Kaprow, Alonzo Ruiz, and Jerome Winkleman all guilty of conspiracy to confound the truth in the act of covering up the facts about what had happened between them and Joe Ben Strother. It also found the three defendants guilty of perjury.

Saturday, Shelby Satik had a chance to talk to some members of the jury.

"At the beginning," one of them told him, "a lot of us thought we should convict Kaprow on all counts. But after we discussed it for several days, we came to the conclusion that we couldn't say without a doubt that Kaprow had acted 'willfully, knowingly, and intentionally' when he had done what he had done to Joe Ben Strother."

Another juror told him, "Sure, we wanted the police to be innocent. Look at them. Look at how they earn a living. Look at their lives. But every time one of us started talking in that direction, somebody else always reminded us about the throwdown. I mean, there was a fact that just wouldn't go away."

Shortly before the end of October, Judge Addison read the sentence, a long one in words but short in time. He gave Kaprow and Ruiz five years supervised probation. He gave Winkleman seven years of the same because, he said, it had been his idea to plant the gun on the boy and his gun that had been planted. He chastised the Office of the U.S. Attorney for granting immunity to Strunk in exchange for his testimony.

"While the sentences I have assigned these men may seem light to some, I contend that they acted under duress, in the heat of chase, and that—because they did—their subsequent acts were induced by panic and loyalty to each other. That while I do not condone what they did, I can, nonetheless, understand it. Because of that mitigation, I have optioned to sentence these men less harshly than I otherwise might have done."

He went on for twenty-three pages in this vein. But the end result remained the same: no time, only probated sentences.

Shelby Satik called Ben Strother at his home that night and told him the verdict.

"What do you think of that shit?" asked Satik. He was on his third glass of Chablis.

"I. . . . I don't know," said Ben Strother. "Somehow I thought . . . doing all this would be . . . you know. End right. That they would know the truth, and as soon as they knew that, then the men who done this to the boy, you know, would be punished. I don't know what I expected. What punishment is enough for a thing like that? But this ain't right. Not probation."

"There are avenues of appeal," said Satik. "This doesn't have to be the end of it."

"Yes," said Ben Strother. "There are avenues of appeal. I know that."

They talked a few moments longer and then hung up.

Satik went ahead and got wine drunk and headed toward his girlfriend's house about ten o'clock.

Ben Strother sat at the kitchen table, doing something he only rarely did, drinking bourbon whiskey from a bottle. Somewhere around ten he went back into his bedroom, searched through the top drawer a few minutes, and then came back out to the kitchen clutching Doreen's disreputable looking needlepointed "Jesus Saves." He held it tightly, even when he stumbled up about midnight and staggered into the living room, where he collapsed on the couch. He had it in his hands when he awoke at six-thirty the next morning, his mouth dry and his head throbbing. When he realized what he had in his hands, he threw it from him as if it were burning, as if to hold onto it might bring further pain than he had already suffered.

Ben Strother

. . . .

October 31. This year of our Lord.

Today at work it occurred to me. I sold a deer rifle to a soldier from Fort Hood. All his guns were at his daddy's home in a gun case in the bedroom, he said. He'd never hunted deer in Texas, he said, frankly didn't think he'd probably even see one. If he did, he was sure they would be scrawny little things, and tough, no good for eating. Not like back home in Pennsylvania, he said, where they were big and young and tender. I only listened with half an ear, like you do; I was studying the guns instead. And sometime before I locked them back up again, I knew exactly what I was going to do.

And so tonight I went back to work after we'd closed down, and in the dim light still left from the sun and the few lights we leave on against thieves, I unlocked the pistol case and took from it a Colt Python .357 Magnum. From the gun rack on the wall I took a Marlin .30-caliber lever action, because they're light and because we have so much .30-caliber ammunition. I also took a Browning shotgun, a 12-gauge pump, and then I loaded a cardboard box with as much ammunition as it would hold. Doreen's Oldsmobile was out back, and I took everything through the storeroom and put it in the trunk. Then I went back inside and squared away the little mess I'd made. On the way out for the last time I stopped just near the bathroom door and looked back out at the store I'd worked in so long. Somebody had forgot to turn the light off in the toilet. I never did like the new store as well as the old one down on the square, though I tried to. I mean, I knew I was just being old-timey, not to change. There wasn't anything I could do about it anyway. I mean, the old store was taken away in the flood; it was gone, and we had the new store instead. That's just the way it was.

Joe Ben and Doreen were taken away, too, but there was something I could do about that. I couldn't bring them back, that's true, anymore than I could bring back the old store, but I could avenge their dying. I couldn't bring them back to me, but I could go to them.

So I drove on home and I got something to eat and turned on the television. There was an early movie on, a John Wayne movie called *The Shootist. That's right,* I thought, *the shootist.*

I never saw the end of it, though. After I finished eating I wrote a short little note to Sheriff Wilson so he'd know I had my faculties about me when I done it. That I hadn't gone crazy or anything. I didn't go into any detail on the matter. I just pointed out to him that I had pursued the matter of the murder of my son legally as far as I could go, and that the courts had agreed that the policemen hadn't really done anything wrong by shooting the boy. I didn't really blame the system—I understood that most all parts of it have to support the other parts of it or it will disintegrate. Although in the case of Joe Ben's murder I thought they went too far in supporting each other. But the end was that these men killed my boy over nothing, and then covered it up, and lied about him, and all the way down the line everybody—practically everybody—agreed that it was OK to do it. It wasn't OK with me; and it was settled not only in my mind but in the courts, too, that they had done all those things. Only the judge said that it was OK for them to have done it all. They lost their jobs; that was all it cost them. All I can say is, a policeman has more of a responsibility than the rest of us has to obey the law. Or at least as much. So, I was going to go to Houston and make it right.

And then I left the note on the coffee table and turned out the lights and locked the door and got in Doreen's Oldsmobile and headed out.

The shootist.

Madeline Higley

When I saw that in the paper about the trial and what the judge sentenced those policemen to, I came to the conclusion that Joe Ben must have deserved what happened to him. Why else would the judge be so easy on those men? So I never felt very bad about it anymore. That I ever thought any of it was my fault or that I had anything to do with it was crazy. I don't even remember what we fought about that night. I wanted to go home early and he didn't want me to, I remember that. I was tired from school was all, and he just couldn't see that. Boys are crazy. Except Donald. He's the sweetest thing I ever knew. I finally know what love is, with him. And . . . doing it is like a sacred act. I never thought I'd be so happy ever in my life.

I do feel awfully sorry for poor Mr. Strother. To lose his boy, even though he wasn't much, and then to lose his wife, too, like that. I heard first it was an accident. That's what the parents were all telling their kids. When you grow older though you can see right through that; they can't take you in so easy as when you're just a kid. I thought there was something off about that. I just couldn't believe it. I never went to her funeral, though Mama and Daddy did. Mama was outraged. She was going to make me go, but Daddy wouldn't let her. "Let the girl be," he said. "She's had enough sorrow out of all of this." He was right about that; I did have enough.

They went over after the funeral to Mr. Strother's house, too, and Mama told me she saw into Joe Ben's bedroom and that everything had been left just like it was before. That there was even this puzzle on Joe Ben's desk that he'd been working on before everything happened. She said there was still some stains on the bed in the big bedroom, where Mrs. Strother had had her accident, she said. They took some food over the next day, too, and stayed with Mr. Strother after Sheriff Wilson went home to get some sleep.

That all seems like another life. I started going with Donald about that time, and since then we've just grown so close. He's finished school already and working over at Fort Hood in a really good job, I'm not sure what it is, and I'm going to finish this year myself, in the spring. We'll probably get married unless Mama is too set against it, although I don't think she will be. I don't know. We may move over to Killeen; maybe get an apartment there. I could fix it up real nice, I know that. I could do curtains and stuff. Then just me and Donald, together. I finally know what love is.

The funny thing to me is, the strange thing: I can hardly remember even what Joe Ben Strother looked like. I can't imagine why I ever let him think he could have his crush on me. I certainly never gave him any indication. I certainly never encouraged him.

Tonight's the Halloween party they're throwing at Donald's friends from work. There won't be any kids from school there but me. The rest will all be older, working and out on their own. I'm going as Little Red Riding Hood. I think Donald is going just as a bum. I wanted him to go as the wolf, but he said the rules were you couldn't spend over five dollars on the costume. I spent fifteen dollars just for the material in mine, but I'm not going to tell anyone. They'll never know.

The Four Policemen

Eldon Kaprow:

Linda is gone again. Went back to Schulenburg and took the kids. Said Halloween in Houston is too dangerous. And I have all this time on my hands. I could have gone with them, I guess, but ever since that happened with that kid, it's no good. About the only place it is any good is a place like Gilley's where don't nobody know me, or the bar here in the neighborhood, where everybody knows me. I think I'll watch TV for a while and then maybe I'll just go down there, to Walter's Friendly. At least there they understand. Which is more than I can say about Linda. I know one thing: I don't really know how that happened that night, and for all the trouble it's caused me, in a way I wish it hadn't happened. I thought my marriage was messed up before! Shit, I didn't know what the beginning of messed up meant. Now I do. I haven't fucked in months. She's more afraid of me now than she's ever been. And it's funny, too, because that took some of the meanness out of me. I can't say I'm sorry about killing the boy, just from my own feelings about the matter. I never felt so . . . I don't know what the word is. But I never felt so in control. I mean, I never felt so . . . so strong, so sure of myself as then. I mean thinking back on it. I remember at the time the excitement, the thrill of it. Doing it. Once you've done it once, they say, and you find out that lightning don't strike you, then it's easy to do it again. I imagine. I mean, *I* could, I know that. I don't plan to. I don't know. If I don't get better work pretty soon I may have to take it up as a trade. It's just like killing a deer. It really is.

So I think I'll watch this John Wayne movie. It's called *The Shootist*. That's pretty funny, in a gruesome sort of way. If Linda was here, that's the kind of thing that would make her leave, mad. If I said that. Or we'd fight about it and then I'd leave mad and go down to Walter's Friendly. Which is what I'll do after the movie, I guess, only I won't be mad when I do it. Just pissed off because Linda's gone and everything's all fucked up and about half the goddamn world wants to make it my fault that it is, just because I shot a thief before he could shoot me.

Well, it's not my problem. And it ain't my fault, either, for just doing my duty.

Alonzo Ruiz:
Thank God I live in this apartment. The way things are these days hardly a kid will ring a doorbell here on Halloween. And I don't feel like fooling with the little fuckers this year. Five years' probation. I can't get over it. And what will that mean about getting admitted to the bar? If I even finish school now, to get into law school. I missed so many government classes this semester I've already had to drop it. But at least I'll get to go to school in the daytime now, come spring, and take as many classes as I want, since I don't have rotating shifts anymore. Tending bar isn't exactly defending the peace, but it's close sometimes, especially when it's closing time. Thank God I'm off tonight. Even though I can't be there to keep an eye on Maria. She's getting awfully independent these days. I may have to kick her ass back out on the streets. Unless she kicks mine out first. I wasn't sure about moving in here with her, but when I'd lost my job I didn't have too much choice. Sometimes you can't be as picky as you can other times. And she did get me the job tending bar, too. So I can pay my half of the bills. Still, it's honest work, and Mike's not a bad guy to work for. A funny-looking place, all that shit hanging from the ceiling, like an antique store. Barrels full of peanuts and hulls all over the floor. It's not the same, but somehow it reminds me of Hip's

Bubble Room in San Antonio. What a weird place that is. Christmas tree lights hanging all over the place, the only lights in the whole bar; cast really weird shadows. I'll bet that place jumps on Halloween night. *El día de los muertos.* I suppose I should buy myself some skull cookies, go to Mass on All Souls' Day and pray for the dead. But I probably won't. That kid. Pray for him, too. What could it hurt?

I still can't figure the sentence. I can see losing our jobs. And I can see getting the book thrown at us. But I swear to God I can't see five years' probation. I mean what are we going to do? It's not as if we were the kind of guys who went around shooting kids every other shift and then planting throwdowns. So how is probation going to affect us? We're not even cops anymore. We won't even be in that situation again. My probation officer isn't too thrilled about me being a bartender. Had to get special court permission to let me work there. Lucky I don't drink that much, or I'd never of got to do it.

That John Wayne movie tonight. God, I like him. "I won't be wronged, I won't be insulted, and I won't be laid a hand on," he says, J. B. Books. "I don't do these things to other people, and I require the same of them." What a saying! What a man. I don't know. Everybody loved John Wayne. It's too bad life ain't that simple. It's too bad about a lot of things. Like Kaprow losing his cool and shooting that boy. He had no call. Good Christ, I was in on that chase, too. I was in on it before he was. I was excited. I was wired. So was Strunk. And we didn't find it necessary to shoot anybody. But that's spilt milk. There's nothing to be done about it. Don't keep going back to it. It won't get you anywhere.

It's late and Maria isn't home. I'm going to inspect that son of a bitch when she gets here. If that pussy is too clean, her ass is grass. That's one thing I sure ain't putting up with, I don't care if I am on five years' probation. My problem is I think I fell in love with that blond-headed son of a bitch. And everybody knows that when love enters into it then everything turns to shit. Ain't that strange? Only, what the hell love is I wish somebody would tell me.

So I'll just turn over and go to sleep and see what happens. I mean, after the last couple of years, it's got to be downhill from now on. It can't get any worse.

Jerome Winkleman:

What can I say? I got behind four months on child support, and I still can't pay what I owe because I don't make barely nothing clerking in that Seven-Eleven. Take my life in my hands and on probation they won't let me have a gun. Every time someone walks in that place I think to myself: This is it. This is where I buy it.

It wasn't our fault. If Kaprow hadn't of shot that boy I probably would have. You just can't go driving off with other people's property like that and expect to get a medal for it. That ain't the way it works with property rights. I guess it was pretty dumb of me to come up with that fucking pistol. The funny thing is, in a way it's all Leslie's fault. If she hadn't divorced me then I would have had enough money to buy me a decent car that I could secure. I could have left that pistol in the glove box of a good car and locked everything up and never worried. But on account of her, I couldn't. So I had the damn gun with me that night. Otherwise I'd never have thought we could have got away with doing it. But I just suggested it. I mean, they didn't have to go along with the idea. God knows they never thought anything else I ever suggested was worth doing. I guess that one wasn't either, come to think of it. But I sure never twisted anybody's arm. I sure never held that gun on anybody to make them do it. Anymore than that boy did, either, I guess you could say.

So it was pretty rough there for a while, after I got fired from the force. I tried to get Les to let me stay with her a while but she wouldn't hear of it. "You walked out on me once," she said. "You ain't getting a chance to do it twice." I never walked out on her in the first place. She pitched my ass out. But there wasn't any point in going into that again. It's just that I was broke. So I told her, "OK. But don't be putting the law on my ass if I can't come up with every penny I'm supposed to pay you in child support every month." "I'll go to the law," she said.

"There's not a judge in Texas that can make me pay you money I ain't got," I said. "And I can't make anything but license plates if I'm in prison. I sure can't make any money." Well, Les is mean, but she ain't stupid. She figured that out right away. So she gave me the time to get a job and get my head together before she started asking about money again.

I haven't seen Strunk or Ruiz either one since the trial was over and then the sentencing. Not that I saw them all the time we were waiting for our swift justice, either. Nor Kaprow. I don't know. It's funny about that. You see each other almost every day at work and you know people as well as you know your own family. And then something like that happens and you don't ever see them anymore. I wish I could have divorced that clean. But there's the kids, there; that's what makes that so impossible to break off. I guess I never will see those three guys again. I guess that's all part of my past, now.

It's funny, too. Because that night out there in the dark, down in Rats Alley with all the red lights whirling around and the headlights shining in the mist and people out there watching us we didn't even know were there. Out there that night, when Kaprow shot the boy and then we put the throwdown shit on him, I don't think I ever felt closer to anyone than I did those guys. There was a kind of camaraderie there I haven't felt since I was in the service. And then the way we stuck together afterwards. I mean, I'm not talking about the law; I'm talking about men sticking together like that, through thick or thin, no matter what. All that old death before dishonor shit. Well, there's something to it. Then that fucking Strunk broke ranks. Never had the courage to hold out against the honkies. I don't know what it was. I guess I'm pissed off at him because if he'd kept his mouth shut. Anyone would be. Funny thing, though; I didn't get the idea that Kaprow or that spic held anything against him. I guess I never will understand people.

William Strunk:
It's not that we can't afford to keep the house now. Suzie's still got her job, thank the Lord, and I make a little extra doing the yard work I do. It's fixing to slack off now that winter's

coming, but there will still be some to do. So we could keep it. Suzie wants to. I don't. I need to get out of this neighborhood before something happens to someone. And it ain't going to be me. I never will understand black folks. How come these dudes got the ring at me because I blew the whistle on a couple of crazy honkies? First they pissed off at me because I'm a cop. Then they pissed off at me because I come down against a cop killing an unarmed kid. They don't ever stop to think things through. I mean, if Kaprow and Winkleman—and me and Ruiz, too, goddamn it—if we can do what we done to that boy and get away with it, then what do they think we can do to black kids? I mean, if that boy had been black, the entire Fifth Ward would have marched on the police department, the Federal Building, and maybe even the capitol building up in Austin. There's just no telling. But since the kid wasn't black, they pissed off at me for blowing the whistle.

I know there's a way of saying it was the wrong thing to do, but I'll be damned if I think it was. Suzie, too. I couldn't never have done it without her agreeing with me it was right. She is so good. She stands by me and she stands by the right thing, too. I kept saying, "What do I owe Kaprow? I don't owe him nothing." And she kept saying, "That ain't the point. It's what's the truth. You owe it to yourself and to me and to everybody who respects that uniform you wear to tell the truth. I never had any babies," she said, "but I know how his mama felt." And then when his mama shot herself, I swear, that just about killed Suzie, too. She went into one of those depressions like she used to get twenty years ago when we were trying to get her pregnant and couldn't. I mean, she even missed work over the suicide of that white woman she didn't even know. "I just feel like I'm partly responsible," she said. "Me and you." She's a real Christian woman, Suzie, and I knew she was right even though I argued against her as hard as I could argue. "Just the Devil talking," she said. "You know what's right, William Strunk. And sooner or later you're going to do it."

So, tonight Suzie's at her sister's house for the evening. A big Halloween party for all the kids in that family. It's probably just as well Suzie never could have kids; her sisters and brothers done had enough for everybody. I hate to have to answer the door and give out candy to all them kids, but it's better than having to go to that party. At least this way they won't nobody burn the house down while we gone to get back at me. If I can talk Suzie into it, we'll move so we can live peacefully. Smart Strunk, they call me.

Well, fuck it. I'll turn on the TV and watch Charlie Brown and the big pumpkin, whatever it is. Them kids will be knocking soon, anyway. I know I ain't going to watch that movie, *The Shootist*. I don't want no more reminders than I give myself on my own.

In the back, under the mattress of our bed, I've got me a little Beretta .25 automatic breaktop pistol. It can't do much, but I've got to have something. I've lived with a gun all my grown life; I can't just go cold turkey. And Suzie knows to get it if the Man comes to check me.

So I think I'll drink a beer and see what that crazy Charlie Brown is doing this year with that dog of his, I can't remember his name. Lately I've been feeling a lot like old Charlie Brown; seems like I can't ever manage to do what it takes to fit in in this life. Suzie says this life ain't the one where it matters. And where did she put that *TV Guide*?

November 1

Suzie had already gone to her job teaching school at Wheatley High School; William Strunk was just cleaning up the kitchen so there wouldn't be a mess facing either of them at the end of the day. The phone in the bedroom rang. Strunk dried his hands on a dish towel as he left the kitchen and headed across to the bedroom. He picked up the receiver on the fourth ring.

"Hello," he said.

"Yes," said the voice on the other end. It was a man speaking. "You and I have never met," the man said. "My name is Ben Strother."

There was a pause.

"Yes?" said Strunk.

"You. What you did. I mean, making sure the authorities got the true story. So the truth got told, is all. I want you. I'd like to thank you."

"Yes," said Strunk. He was suspicious. "I finally did what I knew I had to do."

"I mean, I'd like to meet with you, shake your hand. Tell you, in person. Just to tell you."

Strother's voice was taut, earnest. But it was sincere as well. All Strunk had to do was clean some flower beds across town, work them up good for the winter, cut things back. There wouldn't be any problem getting that done if he got there at eleven in the morning instead of ten. Although why would he ever want . . . ? There was no other agreement he was getting, except from Suzie. All his friends in the neighborhood thought he was wrong; he had no more friends on the force. He might not have any friends in the neighborhood, as far as that went. Suzie was great, but Suzie was his wife. And he wanted to apologize, too; tell the man he was just sorry the whole thing had happened, tell him he was sorry about his son and sorry about his wife and sorry he'd lied in the first place to cover up for Kaprow and Winkleman and what they'd done, killing the boy and then planting the gun on him. Somehow it might make things better, easier at least for him to live with.

So he said, "Sure. I'll meet you someplace. I'm just leaving on my way to work. Where are you calling from?"

"I'm at a Holiday Inn near 610 North and Interstate 45."

"That's good," said Strunk. "I'm heading in that direction. I'll just meet you there."

"I'll be in room . . . "

"Why don't you just meet me in the coffee shop?"

There was a pause.

"OK. The coffee shop is good. The coffee shop is fine. How long do you think . . . ?"

"I'll be there in about half an hour."

"OK."

They both hung up.

Strunk went back to the kitchen, stood there a few seconds looking down at the sink and thinking. His mind jumped from Strother's voice to the trial, to the grand jury hearing, and settled—as it had gotten in the habit of doing—on the night when he and Ruiz had rushed from their patrol car too late to prevent Kaprow from blowing off the back of the boy's head.

"What the hell," he said aloud. "This makes it all a neat little package. And anyway. What that motherfucker got against me? Nothing. I'm the one blew the whistle. I'm the one made sure the guilty persons were punished. Shit! He just wants to thank me."

But still, after he was dressed and getting ready to go out the door, he went back—almost as an afterthought—to the bedroom and got the tiny Beretta automatic from under his mattress and stuck it in his jacket pocket. There was no point in being foolish, he decided.

Traffic was heavy along 610 heading west. Strunk remembered back when he had first traveled the route, when there was no Loop 610 and then when the Loop went almost all around Houston except on the east side, that the traffic would peak in the mornings and the evenings but would be clear at other times. Houston had changed so much since he was a boy. So had he, he supposed. He didn't feel that much different. Partly, he supposed, because he'd had to keep himself in such good condition all those years he was on the force. But he knew he was older and slower; knew the reflexes had gone.

He parked his big Buick at the side of the Holiday Inn, dropped his car keys in the same pocket with the little pistol, and went inside to the coffee shop. If he hadn't been looking for Strother, he wouldn't have recognized him. The man hadn't changed that much; it was simply that Strunk had only seen him a few times to know who he was. He was seated at a corner booth facing the door. He waved slightly as Strunk entered, just enough to know Strunk saw him. Strunk lifted his chin in acknowledgment and came across the room toward him. He slid into the seat opposite Strother, his hands on the top of the table. Strother stuck his hand out. Strunk took it, tentatively, and they shook briefly.

"I just wanted to thank you. For me and . . . for the boy's mother. Somehow. . . . " Strother's voice trailed away, husky but soft. Dishes clinked against each other, against the smell of coffee and bacon and oil refineries. Waitresses scurried about with plates stacked up their forearms. Outside, the haze colored the November morning sun almost red.

Strunk mumbled something in reply, looked down.

There was a long silence.

"Do you . . . want some breakfast?" Strother asked suddenly, the good host, as if he were just there again.

"No. No. Just some coffee. A cup of coffee."

A waitress appeared with an aluminum and plastic pot. She poured Strunk a cup and poured more, too, for Strother.

"There are a couple of things," said Strother when the waitress had gone.

"Look," said Strunk, but gently. "I told everything I knew at the trial. Everything."

"No, no," said Strother. "Not like that. About the others. I just wanted to know. What are they like? What do they do? What kind of person could do a thing like that?"

Strunk twisted nervously in his seat.

"I mean, *you* couldn't," said Strother. "You tried to go along with it, but you couldn't. So I understand you better. But I don't understand the others. How they could. . . . I mean, they were the *law*."

"I know, I know," said Strunk, his voice caught between soothing and impatient. "I know. What can I say? They're just regular plain people. Same as you and me. It's just they . . . they fucked up. Everybody does it every day . . ."

"No. Not like that. No. Not every day like that."

"That's right. Not like that. That part was different. You're right. But with little things. I mean . . . I don't want this to sound like I don't see the difference. I do. But it's really the same thing, the same fuck-up."

"What do they do now? Now that they're not policemen?"

"Kaprow's doing construction. Drinking himself to death. I don't know what job he's on now. They don't exactly keep in close touch with me, you know."

"That's in Pasadena?"

"What?"

"Kaprow." Strother looked out the window as if he was thinking of something else. His hands were trembling, but Strunk did not notice. "He lives in Pasadena?"

"That's right," said Strunk.

"The others?"

"Ruiz is tending bar. A place called Gonzo's. I don't know where he's living." Strunk paused, suddenly looked concerned. "Say. You don't . . . you're not thinking about . . . ?"

"About what?" asked Strother, his eyes both frightened and frightening. "About what?"

"Doing something? I mean, like revenge or something?"

"No," said Strother. "I've always obeyed the law. I've always done what was right, what I was supposed to do. I wouldn't . . . "

"No, I guess not," said Strunk.

They were both silent.

"The guy who had the gun . . . "

"Winkleman."

"Yes, Winkleman."

"He's working in a Seven-Eleven store on Kirby. None of us really moved up after we got off the force, you know." Strunk forced a little laugh. Strother did not appear to notice.

Again there was a long silence.

"And you?" asked Strother.

"Me? I'm a yard nigger now. From police to policing. I cut grass, trim hedges, clean out flower beds. You know." This time Strunk's laugh was sardonic but easy.

"Well, I guess rewards would have been out of line, right?"

"That's right. And I ain't complaining, understand. We all lucky we ain't in the penitentiary."

"Yeah," said Strother. "That's my only remaining complaint. Somehow I don't feel like justice got served." There was something in Strother's tone that caused Strunk to move his hand off the table ever so gently and slip it into his jacket pocket. His fingers probed past his leather keycase and closed softly about the butt of the Beretta.

But Strother did nothing more threatening than to signal the waitress. She brought the coffee pot. "No more," said Strother. "Just the check. I guess it's time to settle up."

After Strother had paid, he and Strunk walked out to the parking lot.

They stopped in front of Strunk's old Buick.

"Well," said Strunk. "I guess I'll be off to dig in the Man's dirt."

"Yeah," said Strother. He stuck out his hand again. Strunk took it. "Listen," said Strother. "I appreciate it. Everything."

Strunk could not wait to get away. "Hey," he said, deprecating everything with his left hand and his eyes. He looked back up at Strother and once again he felt cold, afraid. He wished his right hand were free to close again on the comfort of the small pistol he had in his jacket pocket.

But once again, nothing happened.

Strother released his hand and said, "Well, so long," gave a little wave, and turned and walked back toward the rear of the motel, as if he were heading toward his room.

"Yeah," said Strunk, to himself, alone now. He moved abruptly about to his car door, opened it, and slid under the steering wheel. His hands were trembling. He clumsily put the key in the ignition slot, turned it and started the engine. He could not get out of the place too fast; the old Buick strained, almost peeled rubber, and swung out onto the busy frontage road.

Strunk breathed a great long sigh as he sped away toward Tanglewood and the waiting flower beds.

The day began to turn bleak; gray and cloudy. By noon it had begun to drizzle, a soft thin rain that came straight down. Most cars had their headlights on.

When Jerome Winkleman got to work, it was already dark. He got a Coca-Cola from the cold box in the back and then went into the tiny office at the rear of the Seven-Eleven to get his change out of the safe to set up his register. The day shift was a woman named Adeline. She was fifty-four years old, recently widowed and forced to work for the first time in her grown life. She usually waited around after her shift ended to complain to Winkleman about her feet, customers being rude, the general unfairness of life. Tonight, however, she was ready to leave as soon as six o'clock struck and her shift was over. She tapped her foot impatiently while Winkleman set up his register. She reached across to move the Lane Closed sign from his side to hers.

"Just a second," he said petulantly. "I've got to police up a little and carry some of this trash outside. You've let them make a pile of straw wrappers on top of that butt can." He didn't move quickly as he cleaned up the area in front of the registers.

He put everything into the plastic bag in the swing-door covered waste can placed back away from the line of traffic.

"I don't know why people are such slobs," he mumbled, half to himself and half to Adeline. It wasn't clear if he was blaming her or the customers.

"Aw, come on, Jerry," Adeline said. "I'm supposed to go out tonight. Give me a break."

"Just let me take this stuff outside," Winkleman said. He took the swing door off the top of the waste can, pulled the plastic bag out, and tied the top into a knot. "Where's my keys to the back?" he asked.

"Just go out the front. It's not any further that way," Adeline said. "By the way," she added, "there was a guy . . . "

But Winkleman did not hear her. He had shouldered the tan-colored trash bag and headed out the front door. There was only one car in the lot outside at the front, a fairly late model Oldsmobile Cutlass. Winkleman passed in front of it and turned the corner toward the Dempsey Dumpster that sat at the side rear of the Seven-Eleven building. The rain sounded like muffled drumbeats on the plastic bag of trash slung over his shoulder. The top on the dumpster was down, and Winkleman was obliged to put down his sack of trash in order to raise half of the split top and prop it open. He heard the faint slam of a car door against the rain-spattered darkness. Then he turned back, picked up the bag of trash, and threw it inside the dumpster. He lowered the top again so the rain would not soak the garbage inside. When he turned back toward the front of the store, he saw the black silhouette of someone before him, barring his way.

"Are you Jerome Winkleman?" the silhouette asked.

"Yes," said Winkleman. "What can I . . . ?" And then it dawned on him. But it was too late; he tried to turn to run back around the corner of the building, into the darkness of the alley where he might have a chance to get away. He never made the turn. Two loud, truncated blasts from a shotgun hit him, one right after the other. They did not echo in the damp night. One blast hit him in the chest; the second tore his left arm almost free at the shoulder. The force of the rounds knocked him back and to the right, up against the front of the dumpster. His right shoulder streaked the green garbage bin as he descended. When his head passed the bottom, it slipped under the edge. His body twitched three times, and then it was still.

The figure he had seen only in silhouette turned then and walked slowly back to the Oldsmobile still parked at the side front of the store. The motor started, and the lights came on, illuminating the twisted body of former patrolman Jerome Winkleman. And then, without haste, the automobile backed around, shifted into forward, and headed out onto Kirby Drive.

The car cast a double band of light ahead of it that cut through the rain at right angles to the axis upon which the rain itself cut through the converging bands of light. One could almost count each vertical slash of rain, each elongated drop. Each sparkled and then turned dark as it fell.

Ben Strother had all the addresses, all the information he needed to finish what he knew now was out of his control. He had understood before Winkleman what he would do; after Winkleman's death at the Dempsey Dumpster beside the Seven-Eleven on Kirby Drive, he knew what he would do. There was no need to remember or to try to remember anything; his actions now were in concert with his knowledge of what lay ahead of him just as his actions when he was moving about were in concert with his knowledge of gravity. He didn't have to remember; all he had to do was act in the light of what he knew. And so, without even having to look again at the address written in the little spiral stock book he carried, he drove east toward Gonzo's Bar.

He pulled into the wet parking lot outside the bar, turned off the lights on Doreen's Cutlass, and shut off the engine. In a moment he could see all about him pretty clearly, even with the rain. He knew if he stayed too long, the car windows would begin to fog; and he knew it wouldn't take him long to move.

He had found the bar earlier in the day, just as he had located the Seven-Eleven where Winkleman worked, just as he had located Kaprow's house in Pasadena and his neighborhood bar, Walter's Friendly, only a few blocks from Kaprow's home. Strunk had said Kaprow was drinking himself to death. Walter's Friendly was the only bar in the area and so Strother had gone in, ordered a beer, and talked to the bartender a while. And yes, the bartender had said, he knew Eldon Kaprow; came in almost every night; yes.

Now Strother sat outside of Gonzo's and checked his equipment and his heart and bowels. Yes, he had the Colt Python in his coat pocket. Yes, he had the shotgun, loaded full once again. Yes, the rifle was on the seat beside him with a motel towel over it. Yes, his heart was ready; yes, his belly was ready.

He got out of the car gingerly, trying not to get his feet wet, locked the door and slammed it, and, holding the shotgun down alongside his leg, walked across to Gonzo's. Instead of going in the front door, however, he drifted down along the side of the building, which sat alone in the big macadam square, and went around to the back entrance. Above that door shone a sad red neon sign that said in script, Gonzo's Exit Entrance. Strother paused for a second at the back door, then opened it and went inside.

Since it was the middle of the week, Gonzo's wasn't too crowded. Strother could tell that by the number of cars in the lot; he confirmed it as soon as he stepped inside the back door by the level of noise and smoke. He passed the men's room, the door to which was open; it was empty. He passed the ladies'; its door was closed. Just at the pay phone on one side of the passageway and a dirty white porcelain sink on the other, Strother saw all kinds of stuff hanging down from the ceiling and tacked along the walls. Antiques and other junk littered the bar from that point forward. In a moment he was standing beside the jukebox just around the corner of the passageway, inside the bar proper. Hank Williams, Junior, was singing "Don't Play Me No Sad Songs."

The bar ran along the wall just past the jukebox. From where Strother stood he could see down the length of the back of the bar. There were three people seated at the bar itself, two men together and one woman alone several seats down. Two other men and their girlfriends were playing shuffleboard at the front of the room, off to Strother's left. At the far end of the bar, behind it, stood Alonzo Ruiz. He had one leg up, his foot on a beer case; he was talking to a blonde barmaid on the other side of the bar. No one in the place gave any evidence he knew Strother was there. Strother very slowly and gently raised the shotgun until it rested on top of the jukebox and was pointed down the bar, underneath all the hanging stuff, directly at Alonzo Ruiz. There was no sound but the music. Strother couldn't even hear the rain.

The three shots came so close together that surely only Strother could hear the shell casings bang against the glass of a Maxfield Parrish print on the wall above the jukebox and then go flying out into the room. One of the shells cracked the glass of the picture. Everyone started screaming and yelling, falling to the floor. Ruiz took a little longer to fall than the uninjured people because he had been slammed up against the wall by the shotgun blasts. Finally he fell, almost sliding into a puddle where one foot had been. Then the moaning began, and the crying.

Ben Strother quietly returned the shotgun to his side. Then he reached his foot across to the jukebox and kicked the plug loose from the wall; all the colored lights went out, and Hank Williams, Junior, died away. Strother could hear now, above the wailing, the rain falling on the roof of Gonzo's Bar.

He went back out the way he had come, retraced his steps to Doreen's car, got in and drove away. He turned on his lights as usual, not attempting to hide himself from anyone in the bar who might have tried to see his license plate as it disappeared into the night.

Neon signs and streetlamps reflected off puddles of standing water on the streets and sidewalks. The reflections were mottled, jagged at the edges because of the falling rain.

The only light left burning was on the front porch. Otherwise the house was dark and apparently deserted. That meant Kaprow was probably at the bar, Walter's Friendly. Strother drove there, slowly, carefully, patiently.

This time he left both the shotgun and the rifle on the front seat of the car under the towel and carried with him only the pistol. He wanted Kaprow to know what Joe Ben had felt that night so long ago. He wanted Kaprow to experience the same terror, the same helplessness, the same pain.

Like Gonzo's, Walter's Friendly was not crowded. There were half a dozen people at the bar drinking and watching the television set up high on a bracket at the far right end of the bar. No one sat in any of the booths or at any of the tables. Practically everyone took a surreptitious look at Strother when he came up to the bar, but no one turned openly or looked at him for more than a moment. Kaprow was at the far end, closest to the television. He never turned to look at all.

Strother ordered a beer and studied the bartender. He surely had a gun back there himself, so no matter what else Strother did he would have to watch out for that. It was too soon to let anything happen to him. He still had to get back to the other side of town to take care of Strunk. Strunk thought he had gotten off scot-free because he had finally told the truth. But that's not the way it was going to work. He was there that night; he had kept it quiet. He had helped kill the boy and he had helped kill Doreen and the only choice Strother had was to kill him the same as the others.

So Ben Strother dropped a dollar on the bar top, asked the bartender where the men's room was, and then headed around the line of barstools toward the back. It would do just fine. When he came back out from the men's room, Kaprow would be closest to him, the first man on his right on his way back. He would simply pause behind Kaprow, take the Colt from his jacket pocket, place the barrel just at the base of Kaprow's skull and . . .

Everything went just as he planned.

Kaprow did not have any terror, however, or probably any sense of helplessness. Maybe he didn't even have any pain. Strother stopped directly behind him, extracted the giant pistol, raised it casually, and blew the back of Kaprow's head away. For a fraction of a moment, nothing in the place moved; everything was frozen. Even the picture on the TV screen appeared motionless. Kaprow said, "1640." Blood came out of his mouth, and he fell forward across the bar. The bartender bent forward.

"Don't," said Strother.

The bartender kept moving, reaching.

Strother swung the Colt down and fired, but it was too late; the bartender was out of sight, under cover of the bar that separated them. All the others at the bar had fallen to the floor, covering their heads with their hands, cowering. Only Kaprow remained as he had been; his upper body was draped across the bar, and he himself was now where he would be forever.

Strother thought suddenly again of Strunk.

"One more," he said aloud. "One more."

He dropped his hand with the pistol in it and walked casually toward the door.

That's where they found him; just inside the front door, crumpled up crookedly on the floor. They had to come in the back way because his body blocked the entrance. The other five patrons were still there, all with fresh drinks. The bartender still held the illegally shortened shotgun he had killed Ben Strother with. Kaprow was still draped across the bar top, most of the back of his head still on the ceiling, dripping though, still, onto the slatted boardwalk behind the bar.

Nobody could say for sure what really happened.